A Dictionary of Light

The Rhys Davies
Short Story Award Anthology

Originally from Belfast, **Elaine Canning** is a festival and literary prize director, writer and editor living in Swansea, south Wales. She is currently Director of Swansea University's Cultural Institute and the Dylan Thomas Prize. As well as having written a monograph and papers on Spanish Golden-Age drama, she has published several short stories. Her debut novel, *The Sandstone City*, published with Aderyn Press in November 2022. She is also editor of *Maggie O'Farrell: Contemporary Critical Perspectives* (Bloomsbury, 2024). In 2023, she was elected a Fellow of the Learned Society of Wales for leadership in public engagement and understanding. Twitter: @elaine_canning. Instagram: @ecanning9123. Website: www.elainecanning.co.uk

Rebecca F. John is the author of five books for adults – *Clown's Shoes*, *The Haunting of Henry Twist*, *The Empty Greatcoat*, *Fannie*, and *Vulcana*. She has previously been shortlisted for the Sunday Times EFG Short Story Award, the Costa First Novel Award, and the Wales Book of the Year Award. In 2022, she published her first children's book, a middle-grade novel called *The Shadow Order*, with Firefly Press. Rebecca lives in Swansea with her partner, their sons, and their dogs. She loves walking, the sea, and reading about as many different worlds as possible.

A Dictionary of Light

The Rhys Davies
Short Story Award Anthology

Edited by Elaine Canning
Selected and Introduced
by Rebecca F. John

PARTHIAN

Parthian, Cardigan SA43 1ED
www.parthianbooks.com
ISBN 978-1-914595-83-7
First published in 2024 © the contributors
Edited by Elaine Canning
Selected and Introduced by Rebecca F. John
Cover design by Syncopated Pandemonium
Typeset by Elaine Sharples www.typesetter.org.uk
Printed by 4edge Limited
Published with the financial support of the Books Council of Wales
Printed on FSC accredited paper

Contents

Introduction

Rebecca F. John

'A short story is a different thing all together – a short story is like a kiss in the dark from a stranger.' These words are Stephen King's. They convey something of the short story's indefinable effect, for it is a notoriously difficult form to pin down, in definition as much as in the execution.

Who can say if this is why prolific Welsh writer Rhys Davies (1901 – 1978) was so enamoured of the form, but it seems reasonable to assume that it constituted part of the appeal, given that in many ways Davies himself refused to be defined. The author of over one hundred short stories, twenty novels, three novellas, two topographical books about Wales, two plays, and an autobiography, Davies was something of a rebel: a grammar school drop-out and homosexual, he wrote affectionately about the Welsh valleys he had left behind in favour of London, and is now revered as one of the most accomplished practitioners of Welsh writing in English.

As I sat down to read the entries to this year's Rhys Davies Short Story Competition, I wondered by which parameters he might have set out to choose a winner.

For Edgar Allan Poe, 'A short story must have a single mood and every sentence must build towards it.'

This is reasonable: in so brief a form, it might well be advisable to restrict oneself to a singular time, location, even character, in order to present to the reader that unified whole

1

which will offer satisfaction. And yet, you only have to pick up the work of a master such as Annie Proulx to find enough evidence to force a rethink. Her much-celebrated short story, 'Brokeback Mountain', for example, spans decades and lifetimes.

Is she breaking the rules? Arguably not, since nobody seems able to quite pin those rules down. More often, their effect is described. George Saunders writes, 'When you read a short story, you come out a little more aware and a little more in love with the world around you.'

Undeniably, there is something about the form that, when well executed, leaves you a little breathless, a tad dizzy. It can cause that swell of emotion that great songs or vivid memories elicit. The short story is, perhaps, something you felt you almost caught: a bird in passing flight.

As Neil Gaiman says, 'A short story is the ultimate close-up magic trick – a couple of thousand words to take you around the universe or break your heart.'

How, then, you might wonder, is it possible to judge one over another; to say this story has merit but that story is my winner? It cannot possibly be dependent on a feeling. Well, in some ways it is. But in judging one story against another, the question for the judge is *How is that feeling reached? What decisions has the writer made to bring their reader to the desired response?* One must then consider the pacing of the piece, the structure, the syntax, the imagery, the world-building, the character development. Short stories, by nature of their brevity, must be so intricately crafted that the reader cannot see the hand of the artist.

The stories which comprise the shortlist for this year's Rhys Davies Short Story Competition are hugely varied in subject, theme, and presentation.

While most stories are told from the human perspective, as

one might expect, we have here, too, the voice of the elephant in the wonderfully empathetic 'Pachyderm Hiraeth' by Dave Lewis. Just as there are experiments in perspective, there are experiments in form, as, for example, in 'The Referendum', by Lloyd Lewis, which is presented as an academic paper – 'Corresponding author: [Redacted]' of course.

The thriller-esque 'Scapegoat', by Kapu Lewis, gives us a cutting insight into the decisions people make in desperation, while, in the world of 'Echoes' by Siân Marlow, where 4Get4Life clients can pick and choose which of their memories to edit out, we wonder at who really has the ability to make any decision at all.

'Hearsay', by Anthony Shapland, uses the tiniest of observations to gently unveil a life, demonstrating expert character building in a story full of sensitivity. 'Felix', by Kamand Kojouri, and 'Happy Mabon', by Morgan Davies, explore difficult childhoods with an equally tender approach.

What most often drives the stories included here, however, is the characters' longing: for happiness, for companionship, for understanding, for another chance.

In 'Sometimes I dream about a fish', Polly Manning does a brilliant job of making the reader understand what the protagonist does not, as he attempts to repair an old friendship.

Loneliness and a yearning for human connection, combined with a powerful voice, are also explored in 'Sunny Side' by Keza O'Neill.

In 'The Stopping Train', by Jo Verity, a disillusioned writer searches for meaning in a gently propulsive narrative.

And in the touching 'The Boys on the Bridge', by Brennig Davies, a group of lads united in the most unfortunate of circumstances watch life spin on without them and wonder where they went wrong.

For my winning story, I have chosen, 'A Dictionary of Light' by Tanya Pengelly. This story takes the interesting form of a series of dictionary entries, all of which show us a snapshot of a man, a father, in all his kindnesses and imperfections. It is a gloriously honest work, filled with beautiful imagery and startling truth.

I will say no more about these stories here. They await you in this wonderful volume, which represents a fitting tribute to one of Wales's greatest short story writers. It is a celebration of all the weird and wonderful ways we experience life. It is heartbreaking and life affirming. It will leave you, I hope, 'a little more in love with the world around you'.

And perhaps it will inspire you, too. Permit me to leave you with some advice from Ray Bradbury in that vein: 'Write a short story every week. It's not possible to write 52 bad short stories in a row.'

A Dictionary of Light

Tanya Pengelly

alpenglow (n. English) the rosy red of mountains glowing at sunrise or sunset, lighting the sky with colour until spectators think great fires are burning on the other sides of the peaks, like when you and I were up near the Arctic Circle in the months when the sun never quite sets, in the empty lands of northern Iceland, all grey scree and fjords and scabs of old snow, and I was standing down on a pebble beach by our summer house, oblivious to it being three o'clock in the morning, absorbed in being a mote in a great wonder of landscape, and you came up behind me in your dad-uniform of grey hoody, jeans, grey Reeboks, handing me a black coffee, fuel of the nation, and we stood together for a long time in the quiet, underneath a mountaintop inferno.

blue jets (n. English) lightning which emerges from the top of a thundercloud, extending up in narrow cones, fanning out and disappearing at heights of 25-35 miles, lasting just a fraction of a second, and visible from space as a beam of blue jetting from the clouds, like, I imagine, during a storm over the Irish Sea one night, where wicked weather was lashing rain and gusts up to 100mph, a fast summer storm no one had been expecting, and us camping at the top of a cliff overlooking the sea in our little house-tent made of old poles and heavy canvas, the walls billowing, almost ripping at the seams, and me waking up in the early hours to the storm, little, and crawling out of my duvet, leaving my brother asleep, and I saw your silhouette standing in the tent doorway, your arms held wide grasping the poles to keep the tent from flying away, you all buffeted and soaked, the lightning over the sea behind you, and you shouted above the weather, *Go back to sleep, love, nothing to worry about*, and I was safe, warm, dry, and blue jets leapt up from you, high into the atmosphere above.

corrachag-cagail (n. Scottish Gaelic) dancing and flickering fire embers, like those in the fireplace our family clustered around every winter night in our Victorian terrace, coals brought up from the cellar in their brass bucket, slate hearth warm to the touch, and you sat right next to the fire in your armchair, legs outstretched and cooking, tortoiseshell cat curled on your lap like the little cat you drew in the corner of every greeting card, you occasionally poking at the fire to get it hot enough for blue flames to sweep over the coal, and the sporadic pop of gravel made all the family jump up from watching crime dramas on the television, *Has someone been shot?*

dark light (n. English) the colours seen by the eye in perfect darkness, as a result of signals from the optic nerves, kaleidoscope patterns shifting and coalescing, green-pink-purple-blue, seen most perfectly that one time when you and I waited for an hour in the queue of a German theme park for a rollercoaster that took place in a giant silver golf ball of a dome, I'm just tall enough to ride, and we're strapped in and trundled into perfect darkness to take fast curves and drops and loop-the-loops in pitch black colours, only the green exit signs flashing past to locate anything of geography or up and down, you screaming all the way, *Fuck, fuck, fuuuuuck*, and grabbing my hand on the rail, your nails kept long for playing the guitar, squeezing so hard I bruised half-moons.

event horizon (n. English) an invisible boundary around a black hole from which nothing can escape the gravitational pull, not even light, much like being subsumed by a duvet, while my phone pinged with updates of what was going on two hundred miles away, everything closing down – the whole universe of you – messages from relatives, closer to you, who visited your bedside, held your hand, spoke to you, when all you were by then was listening, and me unable to leave my own bed, sucked in, no escape now, just intermittent messages: *We've been to visit, there's nothing you can do if you come*, then the one that broke me: *I told him we all love him very much, remain calm and just breathe, I thanked him for being our father and for being the person he has been*, and soon an influx of messages from strangers in America, Australia, South Africa, France, Germany, who'd met you sleeping under bridges or running away from gunfights, and me alone and floating, knowing I would regret not going this time, knowing I wouldn't go.

fairy (n. English) a small dancing light, particularly from the reflected face of a watch, which dashes around the walls of a room, but I can find no evidence of this word's usage elsewhere, so perhaps we made it up, *Look, there's a fairy, see it?* but either way, when I was small the fairies were everywhere, and you would make them dance late at night, the light from my bedside lamp sent darting with each flick of your wrist, the fairies were so real, so close, while you told me 'hand stories' every night, where your hand became a book, and you'd open and close your palm to turn the pages, and the story was always the story of my day: *One morning, a little girl got up and brushed her teeth and put on her clothes and went to school...* and, at the end, *and as she was falling asleep she listened to a story that went a bit like this...* and you'd start all over again, repeating the story until I pretended to fall asleep, and when you were gone, lights all out, I'd untuck myself and stand on my bed up underneath the curtains, and open the window a crack to let all the fairies out.

gloaming (n. English) twilight or dusk, nearly night, but not quite, like when I went into our empty kitchen to find your onion soup bubbling on the stove, treacle-thick and salty, R.E.M. playing on the CD player, but you were nowhere to be seen, so I climbed up onto the kitchen counter to look out into the garden, hands blocking out the kitchen light like binoculars, breath steaming the glass, and outside the garden was all black leaves and charcoal lawn, with the neighbour's sycamore filling half the world, bats flickering, and somewhere the cat would be out in the darkness watching them, the dew was rising and slugs and snails were coming out to play, and there you were, down at the end of the garden, past the pond and sweet peas, standing alone in the vegetable patch, visible only by your cigarette glowing orange as you took a drag, long and hard.

heliophilia (n. English) desire to stay in the sun, the love of sunlight, which was always you, with your instantaneous reversion to wearing only shorts as soon as it got warm enough, your factor-two skin oil, your ever-present longing for the south of France, your favourite place, you said, when I asked you near the end, *The quiet sunlight*, you struggled to say, *years exploring the countryside, the people were the best people, I know it down there as well as anything*, your favourite, even long after the French authorities had confiscated your campervan and set you on a train back to the UK, and I was never sure if the quiet longing in you was for the adventure of distant places, the road, or for the sun itself, but I suspect they were all the same thing.

iceblink (n. English) a bright appearance of the sky on the horizon, caused by the reflection of sunlight on a distant ice sheet, often lighting up the underside of clouds, as when our family of four took to the sky from a small airbase in Akureyri (you with a plaster on your head from a dive-bombing incident with an angry gull, from venturing too close to a nest the day before), and together we flew up to Grímsey Island, where the airport runway was half the length of the landmass itself, and the whole place was covered in puffins, but on the way back, high in the air, low cloud rolling golden over the mountain ranges, spilling slowly into the valleys, and beyond that, the undersides of the clouds were bright from the summer-night sun reflecting off great glaciers on the mainland, glaciers which never melt, with wonderful mouthfuls of names, Mýrdalsjökull, Tungnafellsjökull, Þórisjökull, and the largest, Vatnajökull, eight and a half thousand square kilometres of ice reflecting and banding the horizon with bright silver that set us blinking, stained our vision, and you sat there, tightly strapped in, shaking from nerves, you could barely talk from wonder, *Can you...* you start, *can you see...* Yes, I could see.

jack-o'-lantern (n. English) in folklore, an atmospheric ghost light seen by travellers at night, especially over bogs, swamps, or marshes, or when, sixty years ago, you were a teenager, down by the sea edge with your friends all filling jars with fireflies – who saw your necklace of lights stalking down along the beach, did locals think you were imps or the spirits of drowned sailors, maybe? – and you took your lights, so your story goes, into a tunnel in the rocks, which led out under the incoming tide, to a little island miles out, where a lone lighthouse keeper kept his light spinning through fog and rain, and didn't notice the bottom of his tower being ringed with jack-o'-lanterns and boyish laughter, that's how you told it.

komorebi (n. Japanese) sunlight, particularly the beams of sunlight as they filter through the leaves of trees, as they did on that hot, hot summer day when we all took to kayaks and paddled out into deep turquoise water, running fast, and were swept between beams of light, sun flashing, a trip through fifty kilometres of French woodlands and open fields where the cows came down to drink with their massive bulks unnervingly close, and the horses came too, who we fed with sugar cubes stolen from a café, but the word, *komorebi,* also makes me think of how, when the lights were off on the ground floor of our Victorian terrace, the light from you working in the cellar with your lathe and workstation, with all your jam and fish paste jars filled with nails and screws, the light would beam up through the floorboards.

luciform (adj. English) resembling light in appearance; having the nature or quality of light, like the time I travelled across two countries to don disposable gloves, apron, facemask, and push my way through doors covered in yellow tape, *No Entry, No Entry, No Entry (except for prearranged visits for end of life)*, into the Covid ward in a small Welsh hospital, to find you alone in a room, pale and beautiful and gasping for life on a respirator over your beard, to sit and watch your chest rise and fall slowly as you slept, your oxygen levels so low, so low, and I took your hand, warm and dry, and I could see the tiny white scars on your arms from when, decades earlier, you put up a tent for us in a cloud of Scottish midges, and I sat there with you, the room filling with sunlight and warmth from the heatwave outside, the window open to salty air and seagulls, to watch you filling with light, filling with it, and not leaving me today, stats miraculously rising, not today.

Midas light (n. English) the yellow light of evening that turns everything to gold, from Midas, a king in Greek mythology, who wished that everything he touched would become made of the purest gold, and he became the richest man in the world and was gloriously happy until, one day his child ran into his arms and turned to metal, but it was that first stage, the glorious one, that happened late afternoon in the school playground, where sunlight limned everything with gilt – the redbrick walls, the bright classroom windows and eyes and teeth and fingernails of the children playing – and I sat at the bottom of a wall, gloriously happy, taking it all in, the warmth of warm gold on my face, everything beautiful, even the pea-green of my school uniform somehow charming, and then I spotted you on the other side of the playground railings which were flashing filigree like the entrance to a castle, and when I ran over for collection, we were both warm, golden flesh.

nitid (adj. English) shiny or glossy, reflecting light, particularly from a polished surface such as a cut jewel, car bonnet, or the top of a grand piano which is maybe standing in a church, or else a cathedral, or maybe a national concert hall with a crowd of two thousand, reflecting the stage lights from a children's choir concert, or maybe an orchestra, sometimes both, but always with a black grand piano shining and me, somewhere on the stage, in the altos, or the violins (nitid, too), and sometimes at the front singing alone, my voice wavering, young, sweet, and you always crying, and when you collected me from the stage exit afterwards your eyes were tell-tale pink and you'd quietly say, *Well done, my love*, and I'd squirm with embarrassment.

opalescent (adj. English) showing many small points of shifting colour against a pale or dark background, like the insides of the seashells I collected in my castle-shaped bucket from a beach in the south of France, a deep tideline of them all along the shore, open like butterflies, pink, green, orange, and me following them along, greedy for beauty, until I was far away down the shore and looked back to see my brother sitting alone on the sand, not a parent to be seen, so I followed the opalescent line back to sit with him where he was digging down to Australia, while you and Mum were both out swimming in a rip tide so strong you almost didn't make it back to shore, but eventually you both came panting and panicked out of the water and dropped down beside us.

prismatic (adj. English) resembling colours formed by passing light through a prism, separating light into the colours of the spectrum, like the light coming through the south rose window in Notre-Dame Cathedral, all its blues and reds spilling onto a black and white checkerboard floor, the edge of each fairy blended into a gentle rainbow, and I stood for the longest time covered in that light, with you beside me, our whole worlds filled with a magnificent forty-two feet of glass inlaid over seven hundred years ago, and you were never really one to talk about religion or god, or anything bigger than the landscape you found yourself in, but seeing that light reflected in your glasses was the first time I realised there were whole universes inside you.

quantum optics (n. English) the study of the nature and effects of light as quantised photons, mysteriously acting as both waves and particles, which I'll never quite understand, except to know that it's possible for something in this universe to be two things at the same time, like how it was possible for you to be both a traveller and a man quietly bound to his family, cooking dinner, reading me stories, checking my homework, braiding my long hair every morning with me sat between your knees, and how it was possible for you to love me infinitely, while still disappearing for months at a time without answering our desperate phone calls, or how you could turn up late to my brother's wedding, the bride waiting for you in a back room, and how I could be simultaneously so happy to see you then and so, so angry as I jammed a red rose in your buttonhole and steered you towards your seat.

rama (v. Māori) to catch fish by torchlight, with the flickering light scattering across the surface of the water and their little fishy faces coming up, catching the bright air like it's insects on the surface, like in my stream by the weir, the one with stepping stones across to a field with a cockerel, my toes icy in my sparkly jelly shoes, my tie-dye leggings and T-shirt soaked after a day in and out of the water, but it was night now, and the fish were gently swarming and the river sparkled with the light of a thousand string lights from the festival taking place around me, folk music floating from a nearby marquee, the air rich with the smell of cinnamon doughnuts, and you were standing at the edge of the water calling my name, always knowing where to find me, the fish gulped at your reflection, and I hopped along the stepping stones back towards you and festivities and market stalls and musicians and the ever-present tang of cider and weed.

sylvanshine (n. English) an optical phenomenon in which dew-covered foliage with wax-coated leaves retroreflect beams of light, such as from a vehicle's headlights, which can make trees appear snow-covered at night during the summer, such as the time you and I drove to west Wales for the day, listening to Blondie in the car all the way and barely saying a word, ending the day dipping our toes at sunset into the jewel waters at deep-inset Llangrannog, where the life before me clarified from a confusion of school subjects vying for my attention, crystallising finally into A level choices as the water lapped around our calves, and on the long journey back through the dark, the tunnels of trees were all white, frosty, mysterious.

Tyndall effect (n. English) the scattering of a beam of light by a medium containing small suspended particles, such as woodsmoke, fog, or dust in a room, where the blue light is scattered more widely than any other colours in the spectrum, giving a blue hue, which is the reason why blue eyes appear blue, when they are actually the absence of colour in the iris, and your eyes were blue, and my eyes are blue, and all the family is blue, but yours were the palest, the softest, warm shallows, while mine are darker, colder water, Irish eyes, you called them, heartbreaker eyes, you said.

umbra (n. English) shade or darkness, or specifically the fully-shaded inner region of a shadow cast by an opaque object, especially the area on the earth or moon experiencing the total phase of an eclipse, like in the summer of 1999, when the moon slipped in front of the sun and the day turned dark and cold, and I was sitting at the top of a slide in a playground, as close to the spectacle as I could get, enrapt and shivering, and you climbed up the ladder behind me to bring a jumper, and together we watched the halo of the sun's corona shimmer around the black hole of the moon, and you whispered that this was the only time either of us would ever see what we were seeing.

vespertine (adj. English) relating to, occurring, or active in the evening, like all our drives after school, hundreds of them, your desire to always be moving and travelling, taking my brother and me along the coast to all our favourite places, the places from your childhood too – the wooded valley with the old train viaduct arches and a pebble beach near a military base, where we'd watch aeroplanes coming in low above us until we tipped backwards, and the small island with the soft sand causeway which we'd sit and watch getting cut off from a pub garden, and the hidden walled gardens high on a cliff, full of roses and quiet, and the old ruin of a castle up the river, with the wide stepping stones we had to leap across, and that wobbly one in the middle that made you fall – golden evening turning to twilight over the places where we would one day scatter your ashes.

witchfire (n. English) a weather phenomenon, also known as St. Elmo's Fire, in which luminous purple-blue plasma is created by a coronal discharge from a rod-like object such as a mast, spire, or animal horn in an atmospheric electric field, and while I've never had the chance to see it, you told me your father saw it once, a captain in the Royal Navy who went down with his ship when you were five years old, he saw purple lightning crackling around the top communication aerials of a light fleet carrier, and his adventures at sea haunted your life, drew you to the shore time and again, made us celebrate your fiftieth birthday by crossing the Bristol Channel on the Waverly steamboat, the weather so bad we had to pull ourselves up a steep slope of deck by the handrails with water crashing over us, and you dreamt of being a lifeboatman, but you never lived close enough to a station.

X-ray (n. English) a high-energy electromagnetic light wave with a short wavelength, capable of penetrating numerous materials that are opaque to visible light, often employed for capturing internal compositions, particularly within the human body, passing X-rays being absorbed to varying extents by different materials, such as the denser parts of your brain where damage occurred from countless mini and not-so-mini strokes, making it hard towards the end for you to communicate what you were thinking, stumbling over your words, opting instead for listening and tight hugs, or else passing through the Covid in your lungs, the second time it came for you, appearing as wispy white candyfloss, a sweet, delicate thing.

yeoubi (n. Korean) the sun shining through rain, like on the day when we clambered into a dinghy in orange lifejackets and were zoomed across the sea to Caldey Island, a spring day where the weather was fast and fleeting and the rain was hard and the water was big, so big the trip was almost cancelled, but we endeavoured, you dragged us all aboard, and we were taken out across the sea and around to the island, all sharp rocks and sea kale, to a cave where the Atlantic seals congregated, but the swells were so high that the cave was there, and then not there, up and down ten metres or more, the dinghy soaring up and down, and we couldn't see anything at all, but then the sun came out, lighting up the rain first to golden meteor showers, and then the boat dipped to the bottom of a swell, you whooping with the drop, and the sun shone through the seawater, and there were the seals, swimming in the great wall of water, above, beside, below.

zeljónyj luč (n. Russian) a relatively common phenomenon seen as the sun dips below the horizon and the light is dispersed through the Earth's atmosphere like a prism, and a flash of green can be seen for a few seconds, the Green Flash as it is in English, but your father had been introduced to it by a Russian sailor, and it's a sight best witnessed over water, a light which followed you all throughout your life, which you had me looking out for every time we watched the sun dip below the sea, but we were never lucky enough to catch it, until one evening, driving back along a cliff-top road, you pulled over and got out of the car, beckoning me to join you out in the buffeting wind, and finally you raised your arm, pointed, waited, and then: *There*, you said, *did you see it?* you asked, but I hadn't, because I'd been watching the joy on your face instead, flash, and it's gone.

Pachyderm Hiraeth

Dave Lewis

Raj was dreaming. In the distance, he could hear trumpets. The scent of vanilla invaded his nostrils, and the taste of jackfruit and cinnamon hovered on the breeze…

Suddenly, pink and green powder exploded onto the street like fireworks. Gawky men, covered in turmeric, neem and kumkuma whooped with joy and henna-rusted women linked arms in the fading evening light. A train of orange-robed monks carrying jet-black umbrellas scurried by as flame-of-the-forest coloured smoke filled the air before finally, a blanket of soft white petals floated slowly to the ground.

Raj's tiny amber eyes squinted in the setting sun. He awoke with a start, tears running like paint stripper down his dusty face. Next to him his huge mother stood and snored like a tiger.

***

Raj had the largest eyelashes you ever saw although most folks missed them. They were far more interested in watching him play with his assortment of giant toys. If they did comment on his appearance they would say what beautiful skin he had. Everyone loved his cute little feet, of course. And the mischievous twinkle in his eye… Oh yes, Raj was one hundred percent celebrity, and he knew it.

***

In the neatly manicured gardens where every day apart from Christmas Day they allowed the noisy people in from town, you'd see Raj, head pressed tight to the glass, like brown chamois leather, all wrinkled and gorgeous. People watching.

Sometimes the children would shout at him as he happily tagged along beside his regal mother. Her head tilted slightly to the side, aloof, feigning disinterest perhaps, but always alert to his presence. Raj's life was idyllic and he loved every day like an adored puppy.

He'd study the people too. And the different things they did. He noticed they could hug each other tight, like towels or beach balls. They'd kiss cheeks, wipe away tears after falls that coloured knees red. And some would just shout and bicker in those mouse-pitched voices that hurt his huge ears so.

***

Some days, though, Raj would get upset and cry like a monkey. He didn't know why, but something inside him, a longing, a burning; a pachyderm *hiraeth* deep within him... oh, he wasn't sure what it was... but it was there. Like a distant memory of a hot, dark forest all dripping with soft rain, or a carnival of colour with aunties and cousins all face-painted.

And when Raj saw his reflection in the glass he would daydream and hear whip cracks. He'd see flag bearers, drummers, musicians, dancers and singers... Then, a huge cannonball blast, like his ancient uncle clearing his throat, would snap him out of the trance and there next to him would be his mother, murmuring in infrasound and gently tapping his head…

***

Routine claimed his first few years but then one day a strange man came to the gardens. He wasn't the usual man. This one was scruffy, with dark hair tied up in a ponytail, unshaven. He smelled of tobacco and had smooth hands covered in ink. Not like Mr Williams the vet at all.

The man was allowed to get very close to both Raj and his mother for as long as he wanted. He visited six times in all. Raj was good at counting.

Raj studied the man, the man studied Raj. He wrote things down in a little straw-coloured book. Then Mr Williams came to visit. He talked to the man and he went away again with a hint of morning dew smudging his pin-sharp eyes.

***

When it happened Raj was scared. He'd never wanted to be away from his mother. Not for a second. Even when he did find the courage to wander to the edge of the moat, to gaze at the woman with the shiny black proboscis attached to her head, he knew his mammy was always close by.

But on that earth-shattering day, the day he would never forget, his mammy was frightened too and that had never happened before.

Raj was scared when Mr Williams came swiftly around the corner. He was scared when he started talking too fast. He was scared when his scent was all wrong.

Raj tried to burrow into the spongy belly of his mammy but

the men in green overalls pulled him away. He spun around quickly to see his mother's kind face for the final time. She had calmed herself. Now, all she thought of was her only son.

Then the earth began to rumble and resonate below their feet. He was confused when she told him she loved him. Terrified when she closed her huge eyes.

***

For several days Raj didn't eat, until one day he saw a child with an ice cream. Subconsciously catapulted through time he smelt the vanilla pods, tasted pineapples and heard the conch sound from his dreams. He breathed in the scent of orange trees and ate some grass. Mr Williams came to see him and he seemed pleased.

***

Through the cold winter weeks, Raj didn't have so many people to watch. Apart from the robots with long metal arms, the lorry drivers and the men with masks, who used sticks, whizzing with lights, bright as the Indian sun.

A month passed and as the last of the snow finally lost its battle with the wind, he watched carefully as all the men working in the gardens packed up their tools and left. Raj wondered what was under the mighty tarpaulin…

***

'Duller than rhinos', his mother always used to say, referring to the long rows of smoky metal machines that would form herds at the far end of the grounds on special occasions. Raj knew something was happening. He could feel it in the air, like the tang of fig leaves or the waft of incense. Lots of little figures scampered towards him and they all gathered around the giant olive-coloured blanket.

All the people were staring at the huge shape and then stealing looks at him too. He missed his mammy. She would know what to do.

Then an ugly little ape, with a face like a zebra, dressed in emerald-coloured rags and clutching a small bag emerged from the crowd. She came over and pulled on a rope.

As the covering dropped to the ground Raj picked out the man with the pencils and long hair again. He was the only one not looking. He was staring straight at Raj and his eyes started to fill with mist again.

As the monster was revealed everyone threw their tiny hands together, over and over again, and soon a faint hushing noise spread out over the audience. The people were all moving their lips but no sound was coming out as they became completely engrossed in the sight before them.

***

Raj could make out the curved silhouette of his mother but the scent was all wrong. The sculpture looked like an amusing tree trunk, with pieces of rope glued on. His nostrils could taste the concrete, metal, hemp and bronze paint but he couldn't decipher the strange shapes he saw.

He'd often wondered why the little beasts were so enthralled with these bizarre markings, like they were some magical mind map to water in the desert or something.

Raj gazed at the statue…

```
      La
     nd whale           big      and
    mighty. A walk      er, grazer, swimmer, run
   ner, charger, tusker, nomad, rumbler, trampler,
   crumplerofcars.  Muster, violent beast, screamer - a
   gentle growl and roar, infrasound from childhood to the
   grave. With 60,000 muscles in his nose, he's snorkelling
   and doggy paddling home and feeling bones, all dry and
    old from history, spoken, smelt. Touched with love with
      his stethoscope breath, and turned and turned with slow
        persistent stealth, the wealth, the funeral circle, cave  s
         of myth and lore. The memories and the stories pass ed
          on from one to one, the waterholes and saltpans and    th
        e wanderingan    d roaming desert plains and grassland
   a     ndtheju  n    gle forests deep within your soul and
i        nyour   b    ones. A giant vegetarian, gentle, str
        onga            nd brave. Caring, staring trumpeter
        this            colossus beating billowed, billiard
        ball,           the leathered skin, the tender cry,
        the             crescent moon of chain-sawed teeth
        the             men who live      here, kill and
        mai             m, they know       notwhattheydo
        and             when  the          moon  beats
        dow             n and wor            ships    youlike
        lov             ers kiss i            n  g    eyelashes
        our             photog              raphs      only cap
        ture            carving            fractions    of a fam
          ily           man - like         piano keys    of grey
                        perfume de        ep within      your heart
```

When night descended and the gardens became quiet apart from the laughter of the macaws, the clicking of bats, the snoring sheep and the bellowing hippos, Raj decided to investigate.

He snaked his trunk through the bars of his cage but his mother's likeness was too far away. He realised that the steel of the cage that they put there to protect him was now a prison. He swallowed the thick night air as it seeped through the holes in the sculpture before a metallic thunderstorm of emotions surged through his veins and Raj's feet tickled.

He was afraid again like the day his mammy laid down. He cried his lowest rumble but no one replied and somehow he knew that the nearest elephant must be more than five miles away. As Raj stared at the mammoth-sized, moonlit silhouette before him a single marble-sized teardrop began to fill the corner of his eye.

He might have only been a baby but he knew what it was. It was a trap. They'd made a crude, odourless copy of his mother to entice others into the gardens. And then men like Mr Williams, whom Raj used to trust, would come and stick tiny needles into them. He'd suck their blood like a mosquito – take their strength away. Raj had to warn everyone. He decided there and then that he would have to destroy this effigy.

Raj tried to reach out and touch the impostor; he willed himself smaller but he could not squeeze through the gap in the bars. He tried all night but eventually gave up, exhausted, and went to sleep.

***

Over the next few months, Raj dreamed more and more of his mother. He tried so hard to remember what she smelt like but the stink of burning rope overwhelmed his senses whenever the wind blew from the direction of the statue. All he could do was close his eyes until he felt the warmth of the forest and the coolness of the rivers again.

***

Every day for the next ten years Raj pretended to be pleased to see the little people as they crowded around his enclosure. He'd walk in ever-repeating circles to please them. He'd shake his head back and forth. They'd laugh and throw apples. And every night he would use his great trunk to tease the bars of the cage just that little bit further apart. Hoping and praying that one day he could fit through them and escape. But as he got stronger he got bigger and so the gap was always too small.

As the years passed Raj noticed that parts of the figure were beginning to rust, the bronzed paint had started peeling and the dead skunk-like smell of rope had waned. It was finally dying and so he made his decision.

***

It was a fine spring morning when Mr Williams came, much older than before, much slower too, and Raj was ready. He would never forget what he was about to do, just like he would never forget what they did to his mother.

Raj moved swiftly. He pushed the old vet to the floor and stomped and stomped until he stopped wriggling. He turned quickly on the men in green overalls and charged straight at them. He heard rat-like squeals as he squashed two. Another was cowering behind the plastic bushes talking rapidly into his hand. Raj ignored him and launched himself with all his force at the weakened metal bars. They snapped like twigs in the dry season. He was finally free!

Calming himself, he began to move gently towards her. He raised his trunk to her face and stroked the grooves in the rope. Suddenly, all the old dreams came flooding back. Places he'd been, creatures he'd seen. The sights and the sounds of his early childhood rushed over him like a wave in a cool mountain lake.

***

Then, rather abruptly, the parrots and peacocks went silent, and the sound of waterfalls and piped cicada song died away. The bullet that pushed a path through his heart eased Raj onto his knees. And standing there, silent and still, was his real mother staring down at him amid the diminishing screams of the little people scurrying all about him.

Raj looked up for the last time. He trumpeted loudly as he felt his giant heart breaking and smiled as a huge arc of crimson spray settled upon his mother's face.

***

The local newspaper that dropped through the letterbox of the retired artist carried a short story about how an elephant had gone berserk and savagely killed three men in the city's zoo. The statue that was once front-page news was now relegated to a bottom column. After reading the article the old man picked up his whisky glass and walked to the open window of his modest flat just off Prince Albert Road.

He often did this, and late into the evening, when the traffic noise had died down, he would listen to the low rumble of pain that emanated from behind the high wall opposite.

Wiping his tears away he smiled to himself and got ready for future nights when he would welcome a beautiful silence.

Scapegoat

Kapu Lewis

I rewrap my third toe with the bandages the villagers gave me.
'Never forget,' they said, 'your feet are more important than
your soul.'

The skin on the knuckle of my third toe refuses to regrow:
an aureole of permanent beaded blood seeps when I sauté or
pas de bourrée. The second toe is broken but only sometimes
weeps. This is why my shoes are always red. I must not show
stain, must follow my plan to the very end. Everything must
appear as I need the world to see it. Always.

From the moment the paper-dry grass dug into the arches
of my blessed feet when I turned my back on the chapel, Bible
and the mill. From the moment the villagers waved as I
stepped up into the train at the last staging post: thin, backs
straight, like black ranching posts facing my black sail of a
dress.

They had given up everything to buy the contents of the
bag on my back: cotton ballet shoes, a bank note, a steamer
ticket and a griddle cake. Luxuries from their desolate farms
at the bottom of the world where they'd arrived as exultant
immigrants. Then realised they were trapped.

I was their hope all those years ago.

Still am.

I fasten my diamanté hairpin, tie the ribbons of my red satin
shoes and walk to the far end of the boat, a thousand miles

from the Argentinian coast, and enter through the back of the ship's theatre.

'Ladies and gentlemen, from the great Teatro Colón in Buenos Aires, may I present Rosa Riva, prima ballerina! Returning with us on SS Ortega after her sojourn with London's Royal Opera! Acclaimed by the great Pavlova herself when she saw her dance last year!'

Music twangs the air. I glide onto the ship's stunted stage, dressed in the colour of flame, scorched gold; I pirouette, arabesque. The gaslights are dimmed. It smoothes the creases round my eyes, blurs the shakes in my legs, my wobble *en pointe*. It softens the brocade walls, stained with smoke and drink. For I must entertain, create a theatre so utterly enchanting that no one can see through my infernal dance till the very end. Only ten days left, seven years behind and still five hundred and thirty pesos to go. I cannot afford to arrive home even a penny short of the money we owe but there is only so much I can steal on this ship. This voyage among the rich has not yielded what I'd hoped.

The mid-Atlantic swell, rising tonight at twenty feet, throws my body from one side of the stage to the other. But no one sees, for I have mastered the technique of leaping to the crashing chords of Stravinsky's 'Firebird' in time to the howl of the gale and the waves' angry beat. And the beat, beat of my farm-girl soul, free and yet chained by my blessed feet.

And the promise that began it all, the promise that was broken. On a Black Hill. Black from too much rain, the grass drowned in swollen soil, a vertical escarpment down one side, imprisoning a grey Welsh town. The town's churchman created a contract to save us from the wretched poverty of it all. Forty people signed, even their children. Ten years of servitude in return for passage to a promised land. A year later we arrived. On the way three died, but the enduring sentiment was one of excitement for a land made for us by God: across the ocean, at the end of a lonely Argentinean railway line.

But when we get there, there are sharp yellow mountains, frigid rivers, biting winters, wild beasts. There is nowhere to live and nothing to eat. So the ten-year contract grows, because the churchman provides for everything: wood, food, seed and ox. Like God.

More of us die. But we are taught to expect this. Do we not live in God's natural paradise? We all agree, even those who secretly don't voice their change of heart. But the ten-year contract is now twenty. And one day, when a baby is sick with fever and expensive medicine is sent for from Buenos Aires, that twenty years becomes thirty-two. And something breaks, like a mule collapsing under its master's weight.

Now it starts. With whispers, in the dark, two heads on a pillow two inches apart. It develops with a happy accident: a pair of ballet slippers, sewn by hand from wool and sacking, a poor mother's gift to her daughter, who has nothing. The girl puts them on and from that moment starts dancing and won't take them off. And the whispers in the dark grow into an idea.

The churchman does not hear the whispers. Because he has become God, he cannot imagine that someone would believe in anyone but him, so he has cut off his ears, so to speak, for he no longer needs to listen.

Listen: the clapping swells with the rise of the sea and the skidding of unsecured seats. The port side of the steamer lists, a decanter of ruby port (that cheap stuff that lets the light in) topples on the side of the captain's table. A waiter dives, his fingers graze the glass, fail to grab. *Smash, splash.*

'Oh!' A girl stands, salmon satin dress soaked with the alcohol's dirty red. She now smells of fermented cherry.

Silence. Everyone stares. The boy turning the gramophone pauses, my steps stutter.

The girl's face glistens. She turns her head left to right to left, whimpers. Someone giggles, her lip trembles and she takes a step towards the door, ready to run.

I launch into a *piqué* turn, the music restarts and just like that the party is back in full swing: the diners chatter, the waiters' service clatters, the ship's captain laughs.

The grandmother dressed in black bombazine clasps her bony hand round the girl's wrist and yanks her back. 'Sit in your soil,' she says to her. Like a dog on a leash that must adhere to every command.

What a nasty owner. It is satisfying that I have already stolen from the snooty old crone and she will never know: *crocodile purse – 30 pesos, lace handkerchief – 10…* but still not enough. Not enough.

The mournful foghorn sounds. Pointless in this ocean of loneliness. And still my plan unfolds.

The next day the ocean is slack and black. Exhausted with barely a ripple.

'Beautiful.' Warm breath touches my leg.

Crouched between the lifeboats is the sallow girl with the salmon dress. Today she wears chaste white chiffon – a ridiculous choice on a boat that belches soot-filled smoke in hourly rhythm. But perhaps it is done to appeal to men, for she must be approaching marriageable age. Her fingertips reach out, graze my blessed feet. I flinch. And notice the bracelet of blue-green bruises that encircles her wrist.

I walk past her, pretending not to have noticed, I straighten my spine, elongate my neck, point my toes even more elegantly than before. Like I once saw Anna Pavlova do, stepping from the Opera into a sleek black car. I can never point in quite her way; my muscles have never obeyed. But I can act well enough.

The girl lumbers up behind. She has a faint limp she struggles to hide. Polio, at a guess; she should be wearing a brace, but no. A grandmother that bruises her grandchild like that detests imperfection, will pretend it doesn't exist even when it is staring her in the face. She won't give the girl the brace that will save her legs. The grandmother will save her own pride instead.

'What is it like to be a dancer?' she says, catching up with me. 'Grandmother says I will never find a good husband unless I learn to move like one.'

The grandmother is right. She will have to marry off the girl before the polio really shows and the required dowry is not too high. Possible in a continent where a girl can be betrothed at thirteen, and there are enough gentlemen hungry for a youthful taste of home. No doubt that is why they are on this boat. I feel bile rise and a rebellious idea blossoms in my mind.

Perhaps an upper-class girl who learns to hold herself better would have a chance. A delayed marriage, a better match. A better life?

I step out of the shade into the glory of the sun and turn, bequeathing the girl a smile.

'You're the girl from last night,' I say.

She stumbles to a halt and nods, her eyes wide. She leans slightly to one side as if supported by an invisible cane. Her left foot turns in, pigeon-like. Her body is unmuscled and painfully thin. But look at her face: soft and indistinct. She has potential to improve her value. There is a fashion among the aristocracy for the ethereal. With a bit of training, I could build the meat on the legs to better manage her walk; I could teach her to waltz passably at a high-class ball. The girl could look tragically fragile. Rich men love that, don't they? Priceless objects they can protect.

I could teach her the skills I learned in the studio, on the barre, at the rear of the corps de ballet. My dancing is third rate but not my head. Inside it is every move that every soloist and prima ballerina I've ever watched has ever made. Torture for a body that isn't built to perform, but isn't it worth the suffering? Just a drop of that golden liquor could give this girl a little freedom. And freedom is everything.

But freedom has a price.

The days tick, ratcheting up the interest on the pastor's loan. And I am *short, short, short.*

'Would you like me to teach you?' I say. 'It could make all the difference.'

She opens her bud mouth as if I have placed the words right in it. 'I'll give you anything.'

I suggest three hours of training a day until the end of the voyage at Puerto Madryn. I weave our classes around my performances in the ballroom and my private dances for old Allenby, a self-made industrialist who watches with his half-blind sister as he fingers his crotch. For I must earn money to the very end. The steamer ticket, the first-class cabin, the make-up and elaborate clothes have cost me far too much. And while Allenby only pays a crown a time (the rich drive the hardest bargains), he has a gem-topped cane that always rests by his side. *Rose-cut diamond – 340 pesos?* This and the lessons will surely fill the gap.

The girl offers to pay me with a purse of shillings, beaming with pride, and she thinks she is being generous.

'You must give me more than that,' I snap.

'I… I can't. I don't have—'

'You will.'

'I—'

'I am the only person who will ever help you,' I say. This is cruel but true.

I can't believe how easy it is when she reports her grandmother has agreed to my fee and has given her permission to fraternise with me.

We practise in my cabin. I want to practise in the steamer's ballroom, but the girl says her grandmother will not allow it. She says we must not be seen, not alert anyone to the hint the girl might not be suitable for marriage. I do not take the time to ponder these things. The days spin faster towards the end. Time to think shrinks.

The girl is dull, but she makes up for it with adoration. Every lesson, she picks a detail from my dance the night before that she has found beautiful. I have always wanted my movements to be beautiful, like Pavlova or Nijinsky, to make the heart quake. It is a fantasy, of course, but I so much enjoy her naivety. The needy child hangs off my every word. It is hard to resist.

I give her my red satin shoes to wear. She sullies them with her clumsy steps, but I like to see them move. They remind me of the fairy tale of the girl who must dance in enchanted red shoes forever: Heaven and Hell mixed together.

'Neck taller,' I say. 'Back straighter. Don't drag the leg.' I whip the backs of her knees with a switch of bamboo, fashioned from the fibres of my deckchair.

She whimpers.

I whip her inner arms so they learn to bend.

'It hurts!'

34

When she opens her mouth to complain, I slap her face.

Her cheeks flush the colour of rust.

'You are getting better,' I say.

She nods her head, turns towards my cabin door, but I see her demure eyes glint. She wants more praise.

'Kiss my hand before you leave!' I say.

'Sorry.' She walks back to me, her gait at an angle.

'Walk straight!' I strike her across the lips, and they bleed. The girl cries out, staggers back, her face contorted. Lips remember everything.

'You are malformed. If you want to hide it, you will endure pain. If you want to find a husband, you will endure pain. If you want to survive, you will endure pain.'

'I endure pain anyway,' she sobs.

She knows nothing of pain. But the next day, like a dog, she follows my instructions even more closely and the malleability tastes like the first heady rush of champagne.

This must be how the pastor back home feels every single day. Because it works. Slowly the girl starts to learn and obey. If I had more time, imagine what I could do with her?

But the day we approach the Uruguayan coast I am running late for our lesson. Still fastening the buttons of my blouse, I hurry back from Allenby's cabin, skirting the fo'c'sle to stay out of the wind. Yet again I have failed to find a way to steal his cane and the pastor's debt is all I can think of. Rounding the corner to the starboard side I collide with someone rushing in the opposite direction, dressed in black. The girl's grandmother.

'Look where you're going!' she says.

'I'm sorry—'

'Have you seen a girl?' she says. 'Pallid. Green dress. My granddaughter. She's disappeared again.'

35

'Well of...' I let the wind steal my words.

Loose strands of the woman's greying hair flap across her dry face. She is ungloved, unhatted. Unthinkable for a lady of her social standing who prides herself on perfect. Something is very wrong. And my heart pumps faster when I realise what it is.

'What did you say?' she says, looking me up and down, frowning, trying to place me.

I lift my chin, elongate my neck like Pavlova does in photos. 'Nothing,' I say, and step around her. I continue along the deck; I do not look back.

At my cabin I stop, listen to the shuffling inside, then turn the doorknob slowly to ease the door open. The girl, wearing a green pinafore and already laced into my red shoes, is standing with her back to me reading something on my desk. I step into the room. Her back stiffens, and I am surprised she does not turn to greet me like the meek student I have taught her to be. Perhaps she suspects what I am about to say. She must have known it would eventually come to this.

'You've been lying.' My words are clipped like the metal stays that slap against the boat's rigging. 'Your grandmother doesn't know you've been taking lessons, does she? And she doesn't know you stole from her to pay for them.'

She emits a strangled noise. Pity flickers in my heart but I snuff it out. I cannot afford to have sympathy when an opportunity strikes.

'You will pay me triple,' I say. 'Or I will tell your grandmother everything you have done.' I know she will say yes. The girl needs me, loves me. Doesn't she?

She turns, then. There is a raw hurt in her eyes, but she is not crying as I had thought. Her face is full of sharp angles. She holds out the book she's been reading and lifts her chin, just like I always do. 'On the contrary,' she whispers. 'You're the one who will pay *me*. Or I'll tell everybody what you are.'

I stare at the open page and taste the bitterness of my mistake.

It is not one of the modish novels I bought in London for appearances' sake. But a book which tells a very dangerous story indeed if you know how to read it. A tale of pennies and crowns and sovereigns scrimped and saved from every man, every dance, every meagre theatre wage, every item I have ever stolen and sold, and the total needed to save my village of thirty souls. It even includes the final items I need to acquire on this boat:

530 pesos of debt remaining

less

340 for Allenby's cane

190 for the girl's dancing…

Total 94,000 with interest at 1% per day

'Grandmother says I know nothing of the world,' the girl says, her mouth twisting, 'but I know a ledger when I see one. She records our expenses in one every night, while she waits for a suitable man who will accept a cut-price dowry and take me off her hands. I'm like a calf on market day, the deformities hidden. But your money will change that. I won't have to marry anybody!'

She steps towards me then, her pretty blue eyes narrowing in the caged cabin light. 'You said you'd been trained by Pavlova. You said you were the lead for the Royal Ballet.' She shakes her head and laughs. 'I thought you were the most incredible person in the world. But you're *none* of those things. You're the one who lied first.'

Oh, I have been such a fool. So close to my goal, I should have thrown that ledger into the sea weeks ago. But it was my dolly, my comfort, my countdown out of Hell.

Out of the corner of my eye I see the switch that I whip her limbs with during our lessons. Lying a few feet away on the bed I could grab it, beat her with it like the gauchos beat their cattle, make the girl comply with pain. Would it work?

No.

But there's a lesson I was taught as a child that might.

I reach behind me, throw the bolt on the door.

She moves, but I'm faster. I grab her skinny neck with my hands and squeeze. I am taller and stronger than her and I have hands that were wrought on a farm, from ploughing and calving and frigid winters, months long.

The girl screeches, clutches at me, but I press my thumbs in deep. She emits another cry, her body wriggling from side to side.

'You must learn to keep secrets,' I whisper in her ear and press harder, pushing her to the floor. Her tears sting my lips, her florals envelop me.

She manages a strained gurgle, but her struggles are weakening. Soon she will pass out. If I press harder, she will die.

When I am sure she will not speak again, I let her go. A tear drips from my cheek, but I cleanse it. I must not show stain.

I must follow a new plan now.

The next morning, as the red sun punctures the horizon, we reach Puerto de la Paloma, passing its rocky shore and the Faro del Cabo, the last lighthouse. The last stop before home.

Allenby and his sister disembark, ready to travel to the interior. But he does not leave the docks right away. He has business with the officers. The rest of us are instructed to stay on board, for no one else is getting off and breakfast has not yet been served.

We are rounded up, huddled on the foredeck, buffeted by the onshore wind that smells of rotting fish and cigarette smoke. There are complaints from the passengers, haughty questions. Most are still in housecoats and pyjamas. They are cold.

But their questions go unanswered.

The town police arrive. Two are set to guard us. 'La Paloma is notoriously dangerous,' the passengers say, thinking they understand.

'Cut-throats,' they mutter, 'would kill us in our beds.'

But unlike the other passengers, I know the police are not here to protect us.

I turn my face and inhale the South American air, moistureless from the baked pampas. This moment is delicate. It is important I do not sweat. I let my face relax into sweetness by imagining my homeland. My eyes defocus but stay aware.

It takes the policemen two hours to search the boat. The passengers become restless. More complaints, confusion, urgent questions. 'What is going on?' The girl's grandmother, face flat, dressed in black, is brought a chair. The men stand stiff. The women from steerage sit on the deck, not caring if their dresses get grimy and wet.

'Mr Allenby's been robbed,' a passenger whispers and a murmur undulates through the crowd.

When the police return, they converse in a corner with the senior officer. An item wrapped in a handkerchief is handed over, unwrapped, examined. It glints in the dawn light. A rose-cut diamond, the kind that fits onto the top of a cane. Allenby is called over to consult. 'That's it,' he says. And their eyes turn to us.

The senior officer walks towards me, two policemen follow him. His eyes shine like he has caught a prize, for no doubt

Allenby will reward him handsomely. But the officer brushes past me and goes straight to the girl who stands a few feet behind, holding the back of her grandmother's chair. The girl who has been staring at me all morning with undisguised hate and fear. A scarf the colour of peonies is tied round her bruised neck and as expected she has not said a word about me yet. But the compliance will not last.

The officer stops, nods, and the policemen surround her. There is rapid talking, lowered voices, consternation.

They grip the girl's arm.

'What are you doing?' she cries.

They drag her towards the gangway.

The grandmother faints.

The girl is hoisted off the boat, screaming, pleading. I turn away. I hear my name being called and 'Help! Help—'

The cries cut off. Just like they did before. A not-so-innocent faun anymore.

Allenby follows. In an hour he will have paid off the local authorities and arranged for the girl to be married to him just as we planned. The grandmother will have the thieving child off her hands, but it will cost her dearly. Allenby is not the aristocrat she had dreamed of, and he will demand a dowry worth a small fortune. Of which I'll receive ten percent.

In the meantime, the passengers watch, whisper, filter into the salon for breakfast and gossip.

'The girl stole it!'

'The diamond was found in her room.'

'Everyone knew she wanted to get away from her grandmother.'

'Didn't think she had it in her.'

'Did you know the grandmother is staying on the boat? Wants nothing to do with her...'

I get up from my seat at the captain's table. The conversation fades as I walk away.

We sail south-west now. Puerto Madryn is only a day or so away. La Paloma sinks behind us with its rocky shore. I face the onshore breeze. A couple stroll up behind me, debating the girl, the diamond and rumours of a wedding. This moment is delicate. It is important I do not cry.

I curl my fingers round the five hundred and thirty pesos in my pocket. Not much but enough. It is my reward from old Allenby, along with the promise that any lies the girl tells about me will come to nothing. For last night I procured for him a pubescent society girl who will be on a leash for the rest of her life. The deal was easy to forge, the diamond entrusted to me then hidden in her cabin.

Almost everything I once owned has been sold and spent.

Every contract inked on the Black Hill has been bought out. The pastor leaves town, the lines of my bamboo whip across his back.

The months go by.

I take an early evening meal at the saloon each night. Let the wind blow the doors shut behind me each time.

'Gin,' I say. They nod, eyes down, don't utter a word about me not being a man. Don't even ask for payment. They have already learned I will not listen.

For I am their new God. And their debt to me is unending.

I bring the bottle outside onto the porch steps, sit, stare at the sharp yellow peaks, the eternity of grasses bent like old men in the prevailing wind. I too am getting old; and one day the wind will send me away again.

I swig the liquor. I adjust the diamanté pin in my hair.

'To us,' I say to this void of a kingdom that I have bought

with stolen dreams and a young girl's life. I take the diamanté pin, pierce my finger with the tip, put it to my lips, and suck the pain and red blood in. I look down at the shoes on my feet. I wear them every day now. These gorgeous shoes made for only one thing: dancing until my soul gives in.

Echoes

Siân Marlow

FORGET SEQUENCE PRIMED. PROCEED? Ellie's finger hovered over the button as it flashed red.

'Ready, Mrs Harper?' she said.

'As ready as I'll ever be.'

4Get4Life had a monopoly on editing memories – for a fee, of course. With scalpel precision, 4Get4Life could probe people's memories and excise any troublesome elements, leaving them with a headful of happiness and only the most fleeting of shadows for anything else. Family breakdown, abuse as a child, the embarrassment of forgetting lines in a school play or being caught *in flagrante delicto* with a friend's wife. All this and more could be simply wiped out of existence, forgotten, never to be recalled. But that kind of precision required a complex neurosurgical procedure and cost a significant amount of money.

Over time, though, advances in nanotechnology placed the Procedure well within the grasp of ordinary people, and from that point on 4Get4Life had a licence to print money. Selective memory erasure was big business; there were people out there who underwent the Procedure a couple of times a month. It was even something employers offered their staff. Who didn't want to forget all the things that made them feel uncomfortable, sad or angry?

Dr Ellie Winter, research scientist, was a 4Get4Life employee. Part of her job involved counselling wealthy clients before the Procedure, making doubly sure they wanted to forget – and making them aware that erasing certain memories might have an impact on other aspects of their lives as well. Once their consent had been acquired, she and her team of assistants prepped the client mentally for the Procedure. A small, virtually painless injection of carefully primed nanobots, and the stage was set for the final act. Then it was all a matter of getting the client's final verbal consent – all the forms had been filled in some time before – before checking a few settings to be on the safe side and pressing a button to expose the client to the flash of a proton beam. Instant erasure of pain, embarrassment, misery. People had never been happier.

It was all very straightforward. All those unfortunate memories, erased at the touch of a button.

The only problem, Ellie soon came to realise, was that the good memories couldn't remain entirely untouched when all the bad ones were erased. Mrs Harper was a case in point: she'd wanted to erase the memory of her much-loved husband's death. But if she couldn't remember his death, she'd spend the rest of her life looking for him, wondering what had happened to him. The official 4Get4Life approach was to discharge her in this unenlightened state so that she'd return to erase the troubling memory of his unexplained disappearance. And voilà, a steady stream of income. 4Get4Life made its billions; people were happier than they'd ever been. It was almost poetic, in a way. Symbiotic.

Despite her impeccable professionalism, Ellie was starting to struggle with the notion of selective memory erasure. She'd been one of the team of pioneers developing the technology, but in her worst nightmares she could never have envisioned the impact it would come to have on society. People no longer seemed capable of handling negative emotions, and the pressure was on to be happy all the time. *A Happy Team is a Productive Team*, as 4Get4Life liked to tell its corporate clients at sales meetings.

But it made no sense at all to rock the boat and voice these misgivings. Ellie simply had to keep her head down, do her job and remain as objective as she possibly could, despite a growing sense of unease that tampering with people's memories might not be the most ethical thing to do, even if it was done with their consent.

Ellie's misgivings were brought into sharp relief the day Tom came crashing into her office. The instant she saw the look on his face, she knew this wasn't going to be a simple pre-erasure consultation. He began speaking as soon as he entered, not even waiting for her gesture inviting him to sit down.

'Tell me, Dr Winter. To the best of your knowledge, is it possible to erase a subject's memories without them knowing?'

Ellie hesitated for a fraction of a moment, taken aback by Tom's use of the word 'subject'. 4Get4Life's official policy was always to refer to their paying guests as 'clients' – it was respectful, it made them feel valued. Calling people 'subjects' made them sound like lab rats!

She opened her mouth to point this out, wanting to defend her employer, but the words hung unsaid in the air as she saw the look on Tom's face, the glitter in his eyes. Don't go there, it said. Don't go there.

She hesitated, her loyalty to 4Get4Life uppermost in her mind. He was obviously agitated, and she didn't want to inflame the situation further. Patient-facing experience told her to let him talk himself out and then step in, offering sympathy and assistance, and she saw no immediate reason to deviate from this particular course of action. It had served her well in the past.

'So, Mr —'

'Tom. Tom Bates.'

'So, Tom. Why do you ask? Is something troubling you about the Procedure? If you're worried about what might happen afterwards —'

'No. I'm not planning on letting you lot loose inside my head, thank you very much! I just want to know whether it's possible to manipulate memories without people knowing.'

'Well, 4Get4Life would never —'

'With the greatest of respect, Dr Winter, don't give me all that corporate flannel. I'm not asking whether you would, I'm asking whether you could. You're an expert in this field, so just tell me. Is it possible, yes or no?'

Ellie looked him straight in the eye. He was impossible to read, but she knew there'd be no point in giving him the usual 4Get4Life spiel. She didn't think he was in the mood to listen to a carefully crafted pitch.

'Well, okay then – yes. In theory it would be possible, with the right equipment. But it would be highly irregular.'

'That's all I need to know. Thank you.' Tom's shoulders sagged – with relief? That was odd, she hadn't expected that. It was as if all the fight had suddenly gone out of him.

'May I ask why you want to know?' asked Ellie, not really expecting him to provide an answer.

'I believe someone has had my memories erased without my knowledge.'

Silence. Ellie gaped.

'Someone? Who?' asked Ellie eventually. 'Your memories can't be erased without your knowledge and consent. There are protocols in place to prevent that.'

'I don't know, that's just it. I've found cold, hard evidence that I once had a brother, but I have absolutely no recollection of him. He'd have been a couple of years older than me, according to the papers I saw. But every time I try to remember, there's just a – I don't know, it's like a flickering shadow. Like something is in my head and I know it's there, but I can't quite reach out and touch it. Do you know what I mean?'

Oh yes, Ellie knew. She knew very well, although it certainly wasn't something the corporation would ever admit to. This was one of the known problems with memory erasure: clients often reported an unsettling sensation of almost-but-not-quite knowing something, as if the erased memories had left gaps. They'd never quite managed to perfect the Procedure to a point where the remaining memories would leave no trace – it was like taking a book off a library shelf. The scar from the missing memory was always there, no matter what you did.

But should she tell Tom this? Looking into his eyes again, she read – desperation? Fear? Anger? She couldn't tell. Whatever it was, she didn't like the look of it. This was obviously a troubled man.

'Listen, meet me at the Lemon Café at nine tonight. We'll discuss it more then.'

The words just popped out before Ellie had had time to consider what she was saying, and she was slightly surprised at her boldness. Normally she'd never arrange to meet a client outside work, let alone one with an axe to grind. But something about Tom's situation intrigued her. Memories just vanishing? That was peculiar. She wanted to know more, and she really didn't want to alert 4Get4Life to the fact that deep down, she was having doubts about the application of the Procedure.

Just after nine, Ellie gently pushed open the door to the Lemon Café. She didn't know whether Tom would be there, and she didn't really know how she'd feel if he wasn't. But this was one of those times when she just had to go with her instincts, and her instincts were telling her Tom Bates and his missing memories could be important.

She didn't have long to pursue that particular train of thought. Tom was sitting in a far corner, nursing a cup of tea and staring at the tabletop. She walked over to him briskly, surprised to find herself checking her surroundings to make sure nobody was watching her. Why was she so paranoid? She wasn't sure.

'Tom.' Ellie sat.

'Dr Winter, you came! Thank you,' said Tom. 'We have a lot to talk about.'

'I think we do,' replied Ellie, still trying to read his expression. This man really was inscrutable.

'First of all, don't get me wrong. All I know about my brother is that he existed, even though my memory tells me otherwise. I'm not sad or upset about knowing nothing about him. But I am concerned about how the hell my memories of him could be erased without my knowledge or consent.'

This was it. This was the turning point. Ellie knew that this was where she had to make a decision – to trust Tom and take him into her confidence, or to stand up and walk away right now, before she compromised everything she'd stood for so far in her career. She took a breath to reply and then hesitated, knowing that there would be no going back once she started to speak.

'Dr Winter, please—'

'Ellie, if you don't mind. "Dr Winter" is so formal, and I really don't think we should stand on ceremony.'

Tom smiled, despite the gravity of the situation. 'Ellie. Thank you.' The significance of her asking him to use her first name wasn't lost on him. He'd read some of her papers on the Procedure and had a feeling she'd be sympathetic to his problems.

The significance wasn't lost on Ellie, either. The words had been out of her mouth almost before she'd had time to think them. For some reason, she felt she could trust this young man. People just didn't query the Procedure at all, and he was the only person she'd ever knowingly met who seemed to share her misgivings about it. It made sense for them to talk about their experiences, maybe form an alliance. But they had to be careful, it wouldn't do to question the orthodoxy.

'I know we shouldn't say this stuff out loud,' he said, almost as if he were reading her mind, 'but I'm really concerned that people's memories are being erased without their knowledge. It's immoral.'

'Unethical,' replied Ellie automatically. 'We have reams of forms to fill in before we officially erase a client's memories, so skipping all the formalities and simply wiping a part of someone's mind is – well, it's like stealing, isn't it? A part of you is just gone. Like it never existed.'

'Except the shadow of the memory is always there.'

'How – how do you know that? There's nothing in the books about it.'

'I'm not an idiot, Ellie,' said Tom. 'I saw your face when I mentioned it earlier. You know about the shadow, you feel it too. Don't you?'

Ellie sat, silent. This was it. If she admitted that yes, the shadow was always there after an erasure, she'd no longer be able to walk away, leave Tom and his paranoia behind and get on with her successful career and her quiet life. She didn't even have to deny anything, all she had to do was stand up and leave. The choice was hers.

'There is a shadow, yes.'

Now there really was no going back.

Ellie and Tom talked late into the night, leaving the café when it closed and heading back to his place in town. They couldn't go to her flat, it belonged to 4Get4Life and she wasn't comfortable with taking Tom there. If 4Get4Life had her under surveillance – and she was very much aware that they were certainly capable of such actions – then Tom's flat was safer.

As they talked, Ellie began to realise the scale of the problem. Tom had heard many reports of people experiencing hazy shadows in their memories, that awful sensation of reaching out for something that just wasn't there. And these people weren't 4Get4Life's rich clients; they came from all walks of life. They all had these blanks where memories should have been. It certainly sounded as though someone or something was tampering with their memories – but without the rigorous 4Get4Life procedures or even the simpler safeguards, so memories were being left hanging, stopping suddenly and then resuming later with no attempt to make them blend into the overall background noise of their minds. Even 4Get4Life, with all its cutting-edge technology, struggled to make residual memories seamless, so whoever was doing this was simply just removing blocks of negative memory with no attempt to streamline everything remaining. It was shocking, really. How could anyone do such a thing? And why?

The answer came after days of cogitation, hours of surreptitious research. *A Happy Team is a Productive Team*, 4Get4Life's slogan for the corporate market. 4Get4Life accepted commissions from companies to erase employees' bad memories, that much was no secret. It was regarded as a perk of the job, like free fruit or mental wellbeing support, but with longer-lasting effects. But people still had to apply for erasure, they underwent the same process as other clients. There were forms to fill in, counselling sessions, in-depth discussions before the Procedure could be performed.

But what Ellie and Tom realised was that so many people were almost uniformly happy. Nothing ever got them down. It was as though nothing bad had ever happened to them in their lives. 4Get4Life weren't performing that many procedures, even the cheaper ones.

The realisation came as a shock to them both. Memory erasure was a fact of life now, they knew that. But it was a relatively complex task, with all the form-filling and safeguards in place. So how could so many people be encountering gaps where memories should be? How could the Procedure have been implemented so uniformly?

That was the question. And that was what they had to find out.

As the weeks passed, Ellie and Tom were able to gather their evidence. Ellie, in particular, spent many a night rummaging through trial data and memory erasure paperwork, hunting for clues as to how people's memories appeared to be vanishing spontaneously. And what they found was staggering. There appeared to be routine and wholesale erasure of memories among the population, taking not just the uncomfortable memories but segments of others as well. Production line workers felt disinclined to chat to their friends working alongside them, because they had no recollection of having ever met them. Supermarket workers worked eighteen-hour shifts, because they forgot what time they'd turned up for work that day. Farmers remembered exactly when they should harvest their crops, but forgot that they'd never been paid for them.

Ellie was appalled at her own role in this exploitation. If only she'd never helped develop the memory erasure technology! If only she could forget what she and Tom were uncovering – but no, she knew there was no going back from this. She owed it to all those people to try and prevent their further exploitation. But how could she do that? She'd be going up against the might of 4Get4Life and the entire establishment. Just thinking about it brought her out in a cold sweat.

But although the *why* was staring them in the face by this time, the *how* wasn't quite so apparent. There was obviously some way of executing the Procedure over a wide area, without all the safeguards they had in place at 4Get4Life clinics. Could multiple clients – subjects, victims – have their memories erased simultaneously, even? Suddenly, that didn't seem all that implausible.

'There must be something in our environment that's doing it,' said Tom. 'Something that's carpet-bombing people's memories and wiping out great chunks of recollection.'

'Impossible,' retorted Ellie. 'How could that happen? We haven't forgotten anything since we started all this, have we?'

'Would we know if we had?'

She had to conclude he had a point. But even so, they were both still remembering their pursuit of the truth, so whatever it was that was robbing people of their memories, it wasn't universal.

'Could they be adding something to the water supply?' queried Tom.

'Mm, possibly,' replied Ellie, her mind racing as she attempted to cover all possible angles. 'We inject clients with nanobots before we expose them briefly to the proton beam.

And then the bots work their magic – that's our technical term for it – and the memories are gone.'

'But you need both the bots and the beam?'

'Absolutely, yes.'

'So how would you get the bots into people?'

'We inject them.'

'I know what you do officially,' sniffed Tom. 'But how else could you administer them?'

'There are all kinds of ways. Ingestion, inhalation, topical application—' Ellie sighed. It was like looking for a needle in a haystack.

'Hang on. Inhalation? So in theory, nanobots could be carried in the air?'

'In theory, yes. We inject them, though – it's much less random. Injecting the nanobots means we know exactly what dose people are getting and we're able to target the memories we take. Releasing nanobots into the atmosphere is far too dangerous, we'd have a lot less control over the outcomes.'

Tom raised an eyebrow. 'And then you activate the nanobots by firing a proton beam at them?'

'Exactly that.'

'And can we see this proton beam?'

'It depends. Proton beams are usually invisible, although they may create a visible glow when they come into contact with certain materials.'

'And would they glow when they come into contact with human bodies, say? Or nanobots?'

'Unlikely.'

'Then, Dr Winter, follow me. I think I have an idea.'

Ellie did as she was told. Tom wasn't as immersed in the technology as she was, so he could give his imagination free rein as he considered the possibilities. As one of the original developers of the technology, she knew better than most how the erasure mechanisms worked – but that also limited her perspective to known solutions and concepts in development. Tom, however, had no such restrictions imposed on him, and his imagination was working overtime.

They took the tram into town, jostling alongside commuters, people going shopping, heading for school. They all looked so carefree, Ellie noted, just going about their days and getting on with their lives. Until that day Tom walked into her office, she'd never stopped to wonder why.

Jumping down from the tram, Tom took her hand. It was important to keep up appearances, he said. They had to blend in with everyone else, and that meant hand-holding, smiling faces. Ellie concurred, though her smile was slightly forced. She was still feeling the weight of the recent revelation, the knowledge of her part in all this – dysfunction.

'Look up,' said Tom, stopping suddenly. 'What do you see?'

Ellie gazed upwards, seeing nothing remarkable about the urban landscape. Buildings, street lamps, telephone masts, roof after roof extending down the street. All so normal.

'Look again.'

'I see – nothing untoward?' she ventured, nervous without really knowing why. What on earth was Tom thinking?

'Look carefully at every building. What do they all have in common?'

'Oh! I see. Burglar alarm siren boxes. They all have them.'

'And all those alarms are made by – ?'

'CCure4Life. It's a subsidiary of 4Get4Life. So?'

Tom rolled his eyes. For such an intelligent woman, she could be incredibly dense at times.

'Could those siren boxes actually be firing proton beams towards street level?'

Ellie stopped in her tracks. In an instant, she realised Tom may well be onto something. Invisible proton beams, fired at people just going about their daily lives. If they had no nanobots in their systems, they'd never know anything was happening. But when they were carrying a nanobot load, the beams would be triggering those bots, sending them instantly brainwards to complete their destructive task. It was astonishingly simple, and so plausible. Surely it couldn't be that straightforward?

As they passed an alleyway, Tom suddenly grabbed Ellie by the arm and yanked her aside, pinning her up against a wall and whispering urgently in her ear.

'Just pretend we're a couple. Don't say anything.' Ellie nodded, dumbstruck. 'I think this is what's happening. People are inhaling the nanobots when they're at work, and when they're out and about the proton beams are being fired at them. They forget all kinds of things, they're all perma-happy, work rates go through the roof, companies make shedloads of money. Now, I'm going to kiss you briefly, just in case anyone is watching and wondering what we're up to. I know you're a bit older than me, but there's no law against that! And then we're going to laugh and walk away, hand in hand. Ready?'

Despite the sinking feeling in the pit of her stomach as she realised everything Tom said was perfectly plausible, Ellie smiled as his lips met hers. It had been a very long time since she'd shared any form of intimacy with anyone – the job came first. And despite the fluttering in her tummy, she knew something had to be done about the erasure, and she knew it had to be done very soon. The thought filled her with trepidation.

Confirming Tom's suspicions proved to be astoundingly simple. Ellie just 'borrowed' a portable scintillation detector from the lab one evening, concealing it in her pocket, then ducking into doorways away from the ever-watchful eyes of the security cameras and checking the readings. It wasn't hard to confirm the presence of proton beams. Very low-level beams, emitted as the briefest of intermittent flashes. Not enough to cause lasting, or even noticeable injury, but enough to trigger the nanobot initiation sequence that led to wholesale erasure of memories. Ellie was floored – how could anyone take this incredible technology that had been developed to help people live happier lives, and use it so indiscriminately, so carelessly?

She felt the tears pricking her eyes as she considered all the happy moments lost, irretrievably, from people's lives. Memories of children, spouses, pets. The happiest of moments. All wiped out in pursuit of corporate greed. Striving for maximum efficiency at minimal cost.

Tom, realising the depth of her regret about the part she'd played in this human tragedy, was on hand whenever she needed it, providing a listening ear as she cried and raged, impotent to alter any aspect of the situation that they could now assume was widespread.

Or was she?

Ellie's position as an eminent research scientist meant she regularly gave lectures and presentations setting out advances in erasure technology and ways of streamlining the Procedure. It was this high profile that had brought Tom to her office that day all those months ago, knowing that she of all people would be aware of the possible mechanisms that could be used to erase people's memories without their knowledge.

But Ellie's doubts about the Procedure were something Tom

couldn't possibly have known about. Musing on just how ethical it was to take away people's memories, even for the most humane of reasons, kept Ellie awake at night. What right did anyone have to play God with human emotions? Who could say what memories people should be 'allowed' to keep, what they should forget? It was bad enough that 4Get4Life tampered with people's memories at their request, but erasing memories so that people could work harder, cost less – that was just immoral. It was slavery. And it had to stop.

With all these thoughts ringing inside her head, Ellie prepared her official lecture as keynote speaker for the sixth annual 4Get4Life Memory Erasure Symposium, an event that attracted a great deal of media attention. She normally dreaded these events, especially as they were livestreamed all over the world. But she'd never dreaded an event quite as much as this one. This speech would define the rest of her life. And possibly shorten it considerably.

Stepping up to the podium to ringing applause, Ellie swallowed hard. This was it, this was the moment she and Tom had spent the last months working towards. Her hands felt clammy, leaving sweaty prints on the sheets of paper that she was planning to ignore just as soon as she got into her stride.

Clearing her throat, her eyes roamed over the assembled audience. She recognised many of the faces, colleagues whom she'd worked with for years, acquaintances working in other departments, so many people. And there, sitting almost in the middle and five or six rows back, was Tom. The man who'd started off this whole hunt for the truth, the man with the suspicions and the wherewithal to do something about them. 4Get4Life claimed to make people's lives better, she thought – but when it really came down to it, Tom was the one person who truly had their best interests at heart. He didn't want people to lose all their memories of the things that gave them their personalities, their lives. And that, to her, was a far more noble cause than helping people to live happier lives by simply wiping out the negatives as if they'd never existed.

Taking a deep breath, her eyes fixed firmly on Tom's face, Ellie began to speak.

The fallout came with surprising speed as people all over the world suddenly became aware that their memories, the very core of their being, were being manipulated by others. Corporations, public authorities – so many organisations with only their own interests at heart were using the technology spearheaded by Ellie and her colleagues to improve efficiency, save money. And not one of them had queried just how ethical their approaches were. Not one of them counted the human cost of their wholesale erasure of memories.

The calls for legal action came next. Lawsuits running into billions, group actions, litigation spurred by a desire for recompense and revenge for all the moments lost, never to be recovered. But more importantly, the collective public outrage at the liberties taken with their very thoughts was leading to demands for greater regulation of memory erasure technology – this could never be allowed to happen again. If organisations couldn't be trusted not to abuse the trust placed in them to do the right thing with the immense power at their fingertips, then that power would simply have to be curtailed.

Ellie and Tom stood and watched as the world as they knew it collapsed around them, memory erasure technology discredited. They derived no satisfaction from watching organisations – and 4Get4Life – pay the price for their actions, knowing that millions of people's lives had been irrevocably blighted by the indiscriminate use of the technology. Though they knew that thanks to Tom's visit to Ellie's office that day, their tenacious investigations leading to the discovery of the covert proton beam transmitters, the Procedure would now have to be redefined for use only in very restricted circumstances. From this point on, people would just have to relearn how to cope with their negative emotions and take the bad as the price they paid for the good. There would, of course, still be applications for memory erasure, but such widespread use would never again be permitted.

When the dust had eventually settled, Tom became an advocate for victims of memory manipulation. Their memories could never be restored, he knew, but he could help them to come to terms with their situations and encourage them to make new memories. They just had to find the courage to move forward with their lives and accept the aspects that shaped their futures, both good and bad. It was all part of what it meant to be human, after all.

Ellie, for her part, still had work to do. Although she'd left 4Get4Life, her new employer asked her to put together a team of researchers tasked with developing technology to restore memories erased by the Procedure, and initial trials were looking promising. And alongside this very important initiative, she worked on overseeing the establishment of an ethics committee to safeguard against future abuses of memory erasure technology. Never again would this be allowed to happen. The erasure technology genie was well and truly out of the bottle and would never be forced back in, but the world could learn to control it and use it for beneficial purposes, harnessing its capabilities and enhancing wellbeing in society. Crime victims or bereaved parents would still be able to elect to wipe their painful memories, but no longer would it be possible to just do away with aspects of people's pasts – and consent was now key. There would be no more covert erasure; by law all procedures had to be performed with the full knowledge and cooperation of the subject.

Some months later, Ellie was writing a paper on memory recovery. In a moment of distraction, she glanced out of her office window and watched people passing by. A couple of them looked quite glum, she thought. How strange. In this day and age, what on earth did people have to be miserable about? She really couldn't remember the last time she'd felt like that.

Hearsay

Anthony Shapland

Sun-warm, the pebble is blue-grey and smooth, large in his small fingers. He is sure it will taste good. It rests salt-slicked on his tongue and he sucks his cheeks and rolls it round and round. He squints at the dazzling sea and pushes hot sand through his toes in glee.

Suddenly, it's gone.

He looks at his empty hands, mouth open, puzzled. Grown-ups look angry, or worried. He can't tell. They scare him, ask him if he swallowed it and push fat fingers past his gums.

He shakes his head and looks away, mute, until they leave him alone.

He fuels his nightshift with junk food. Easy. Savoury. Sweet.

The sun rises though the night hasn't left his body. Icy, he sits waiting. Outside is a fresh spring morning, inside, washing dries on radiators. Air hangs, humid with oily tea towels and damp underwear.

Night starts at seven in the morning for him; his working day at seven in the evening. Night for day for night. A life upside-down, a counterpoint – busy while others quietly rest. He no longer likes it, the wait for the silence. He is the echo, the last noise.

Nocturnal years of work pass, daylight fades those he knew, those who live in the sun. Month by month his whole body grows more tired and month by month by year he grows more alone. And so, to bed again. Limbs rest heavy on sheets in a familiar comedown, blood rushes a beat through his ear into the pillow and his eyes close. Sleep drops him through space, a long descent through gentle clouds.

Abruptly, this time he brakes, mid-air.

A flash and the sheen of plumage and bright brown eyes.

A starling tilts its head three quarters, its eye fixed. It can't see him, only its own reflection, but still it watches. He is unused to being looked at and feels held in its gaze.

Slowly he sits up.

The bird hops, sensing movement, walks with a roll to the ledge. Wings-spread-arrow-swift gone.

Sleep is broken in the distraction. The starling appears, with twigs, tucking under the eaves of the steep pitch. Then again, carrying grass, then string, then sticks, too-big. It comes and goes all day. From above he looks down as it hops in and out of a half-built nest. Every time his eyes open from slumber, there is progress nearby. His mind drifts in the rhythm of the small bird.

He wakes in the early evening gloom and moves cautiously toward the window. A new ragged shape sits in the dark eaves that frame the room. Excited, he peers for movement but finds none.

He clicks the light switch and the view outside disappears. Silverfish, like uncertain punctuation, find cover beneath the lino. He looks back at his reflection, the bare room beyond, and all at once he feels himself an object amongst objects, no more or less important.

His eyes trace the horizon. Orange streetlights mark his too-familiar route to work.

Every night he descends the narrow stairs to his shift, alone. A basement room crackling with static, a bank of screens. He locks himself in. From here he is the eye, the security guard in the darkening green night-vision view of the town. He settles into the monitoring station, awkward in the ergonomic seat that quickly makes his back ache.

He is so used to scanning screens that he no longer focuses. He looks wide, the edges of his vision twitch and register. Everything happens, nothing happens. All the time.

Each screen blinks in a rhythm following the other, and lights ripple through the soothing darkness. So many connections sweep across the monitors. He thinks of the starling, at the edges of a murmuration as it pulls and stretches the flock, following, guiding. A ricochet back and forth of movements and turns.

He waits for glitches in the pattern onscreen, the start of any change in behaviour, in direction. Night after night people pass through. A woman smokes in a bus shelter on camera four beneath a spider that ghosts a net of threads. On eight, a couple kiss. He looks away. The narratives of other lives, of all life.

On camera eleven, moths circle security lamps in pale scribbles and arcs. A dogwalker glows by phone-light.

He watches how people behave, walk, interact. How do they understand each other? How are they not shy, not awkward?

Camera sixteen looks out past the pier to sea, the last glow of sunset burns the pixels of the horizon pale green. The bright dot of a cargo ship moves from left to right.

Below camera three, rain bounces off the bare head of a man pissing in a doorway. The stream hits the wall, bubbles in a downpour of froth to the gutter. The man hunches, zips, sways offscreen to walk through the lens of camera twenty-two.

Dreamlike, everything connects as he watches. He responds, mirrors people – finds he is smiling when they smile. There and not there, he borrows interactions that pass through this grid and disappear. In this pattern he feels less friction with the world. He flows with it.

He stares at the cooling tower that breathes soft, digital sighs. The hum of sequences and pulses loop and flicker, the green *on* light turns to a red *standby*. From the fans, warm, dry air whirrs like flying insects around his face.

He stares at the curtains moving. Street noise finds him in the stuffy flat under morning sun, demanding and insistent, pushing into his awareness and tightening a grip. He's on standby, waiting for the long blink of sleep, numb. His ears pick out a different sound.

The starling.

It pours out a mating song; from crystal to gravel and back, guttering sounds and coos and peeps flow in variations of a refrain. From his pillow he watches the flutter of its throat. The starred green shine of its dark feathers and the graceful awkward shift and sway, foot to foot.

His phone rings. He taps it, but the screen is blank. Uncharged. The ringtone continues and nothing makes sense. It goes on. He presses buttons to make it stop. It stops.

Then starts again, a phrase repeated, strident, pure and clear in amongst guttering clicks and rattles. Unmistakeable. Electronic. It is the bird. The gentle trill of its beak summoning those sounds. He laughs in wonder.

The starling side-eyes, its chorus interrupted. It knows, he thinks. It knows, as I know.

The bird dives into the void, fast toward the others. A tilt of a wing ripples through the flock and they turn together, lift together. The breaks in the pattern are cause and consequence; one thing, just as the mosaic of his screens is one thing, one moving repeating motion.

Those parts of his world are signalled, called, sung out to him.

The window stays open. The sill is shared with the new pair and he watches from his bed. The starlings feather the nest, there at the apex of the house by his pillow. Above everything, they three.

He sits apart from his own tiredness and it feels solid and separate from his body. His weariness becomes a thing to be examined, like hunger or lust. All of those things that seemed before to govern him feel outside. Sleeplessness and the day's clumsiness are far away and he lies awake crooning softly. A mimic's mimic, he whistles his own ringtone.

In his mouth, like the pebble. A voice not his own. At school, the sounds that fell from him were always wrong. They drop like weights on his teacher's patience until he mimics the right sounds and says what he hears —

A not A
O not *O*
t-t-t-t-t-t-t. On its own, *ff* not *v*

Ch-Ch-Ch-Ch for Christ's sake, *ch* like chair.

He shrinks. He makes himself quieter and they seem not to notice. His accent copies their accent, his voice disappears and he blends in.

He learns the different round sounds. Rehearsal makes it easier. He learns what to say, hears the rhythm of noise that pushes patter back and forth. Small talk. A tongue full of their speech. He lets conversation peter out until he can be alone.

With his head on the pillow, he gently whistles phrases. Imitates the voice of the starling. Sings the melody and the dips and pauses. A serenade. The rhythm comes easy. The conversation sustains.

He doesn't doubt he sleeps, but it feels dreamless. He doesn't doubt he dreams, but dreams feel the same as being awake. He sees five pale blue eggs and gazes at plumage dotted with stars and whistles gentle joy.

He remembers that pebble. He's never sure it left his body.

The noise from the nest changes. Insects and berries arrive in a constant relay. He puts what he can find on the sill, scraps chopped small and the gulp-stoppered *wheepwheep* pauses. As summer arrives, the high-pitched noises become voices.

With each passing day, the desire to perform sleep lessens. He feels reluctant to crease the well-made bed, to dent the pillow when his head is so light on his shoulders, but he does.

He sings to himself, to them, repeating the five notes of music with hope they may be sung back to him. Soon the nestlings fledge. He watches them being fed, open yellow-red mouths, wings fanned. Lifting.

He feels a pull to vertical, whenever he sits down, anxious at their reach and loll at the edge of the roof. Moving is a strange sensation. It's a numb echo of himself, as though his mind is late in telling him what to do. His hands pick things up before he is aware he is going to reach out. His body is a strange vessel he can't steer, it feels outside of him, beyond his control.

The fledglings squabble and call to each other, as they trapeze into the sky and back. Beaks wide for more food. The eggshells left behind, pale blue and empty.

He wonders if one day he'll pass that pale blue pebble. Whether he'll shit it, body-warm, to ricochet down through all five storeys below, shattering the old pipes buried deep in the yellow clay.

The starlings stop coming.

He sits and watches. He whistles the phrase, those five notes, and waits to hear it returned.

Sleep stops coming.

The chatter gets closer and louder. He stands at the window, as, in chorus, they sweep up to roost in numbers. They gather on the roof of the house, covering every surface, and the song ripples through hops and arcs of chatter. TV aerials sway and bow.

He looks out, awkward on his feet. He feels like he shouldn't be standing inside, but high above the flat, where he could see more and understand.

He senses their magnetic pull, as they lift from the roof and swoop into dusk.

They take his wide-eyes in loops at the horizon and return and roll, hypnotically, until he slides into sweet sleep and smiles, buoyed, floating high and soaring – and, for one weightless moment –

he is flock.

Felix

Kamand Kojouri

My name is Felix Hahn. Felix means happy. Hahn means rooster. Mama says I wasn't a happy baby when I was born, but she thought *Happy Rooster* would be funny. Ha ha.

Mrs Balashova says I have to stop pretending Mama's still here. Have to stop saying 'Mama says' or 'Mama is'. She says I'm in 'denial', but Mrs Balashova doesn't understand two things:

1. I'm <u>not</u> in denial: Mama was killed in a train station and the man who killed her opened a case and took out a violin. He played for an hour before he pulled out his gun and killed six people. Mama was the sixth.

2. When a person dies, they don't stop saying or being. Only, we can't hear, see, or touch them. For example: if you make an extraordinary high-pitched fart (68 kHz), I won't be able to hear it, but a cat will and he'll probably scratch your eyes out, especially if the fart is eggy and you're in a small room with no windows.

The one thing Mrs Balashova <u>does</u> understand is German. Apparently, she's the only one in the entire school who speaks German, and since German is the only language I speak, the kids in my school won't know how clever I am.

Anya, my grandmother, doesn't speak German either, but she doesn't speak to me in Russian like everyone else because she's intelligent and knows I don't speak it. There's a weird silence when she tries to tell me something. Sometimes a soft sound escapes her mouth as she gestures a long sentence to me, and this makes me think she's mute and I'm deaf.

Anya doesn't look anything like Mama. She is softer and rounder. Mama was taller, but she is very pretty. I say 'Mama *was* taller' because there's no set timeframe for when skeletonisation occurs, which is the last stage of human decomposition. Did you know that if Mama was pregnant with me when she died, she could've still given birth to me because the extreme pressure of her intra-abdominal gases would force her uterus out? I would be dead, of course, which isn't scary, just strange, because a dead Mama would give birth to a dead Felix. You see, you must think about these things because if you don't think about them then you'll never know, and even more important, you won't know that you don't know.

Seven days after Mama died, Papa told me he was taking me to Russia to live with Anya. The words reached me, but they didn't stop to be understood, they just continued to go out of the room.

I've been living with Anya for 79 days now and this is everything I know about her:

1. Anya never leaves the house. She does her grocery shopping over the phone.

2. Every month, Anya buys clothes from a magazine. She tells me to choose clothes for myself too. Last month, we bought enough to receive a free gift. She let me select a small grey radio.

3. Anya didn't hug me when she saw me for the first time (78 days ago). She patted my head like you do to a dog (that you like).

4. Anya always smells of soap (which makes her my favourite grandmother so far).

5. I would rate her cleanliness as 7, her friendliness as 7, and her food as 6. I am very <u>alone</u> here.

6. Anya's house isn't very big. When you step into her house, you enter the living room and smell lamb and onions and dust. The room closest to the door is the kitchen and there's a room next to that (that's always locked). If you walk across the living room and pass the narrow hall, you get to two rooms. Anya's room is on the left, mine's on the right. My room used to belong to Mama, which is how I know I'm meant to be here, sleeping on Mama's bed and putting my things neatly on Mama's dresser. There's a lemon balm on the dresser that I always smell before I sleep (because it must've belonged to Mama), and then I tighten the lid counting 1,2,3 in my head. Before, I used to count 1,2,3 only three times, but after <u>the worst day of my life</u> it became 1,2,3 three times multiplied by 3, and it can reach up to more and more multiples of 3. But then I remember: *Felix Felix Felix*, and Felix means happy, so I put the balm back on the dresser and lie on the bed. I close my eyes and imagine Mama laughing.

I didn't want to wake up today (August 15) for two reasons:

1. It's the first time I got older without Mama.

2. Anya doesn't know it's my birthday, so there'll be no cake.

But I still woke up today (August 15), <u>even though I didn't want to</u>, and carried out my rituals. I made my bed, washed my face, brushed my teeth, and wore the white shirt that Mama says makes me look like a young blond Alain Delon. I sat at my desk, switched on my desk lamp, and brought out my plastic compass. I used the mirror on the back of the compass to inspect the dark birthmark on my chest (this one is a <u>yearly ritual</u> because Dr Müller told me it might grow as I get older, which is dangerous). I measured it with my grey ruler and wrote it in my notebook, comparing the measurements from the past three years. It didn't grow! Hurrah! I opened the drawer where I keep all my prized possessions. On the very top, I've placed the cinema ticket from when Mama took me to see my first film in the cinema (*Pappa Ante Portas*). It was a funny film and Mama's laugh was like a torch in the dark. The second thing I have is Mama's watch. I asked if I could keep it after Papa smashed the glass. It still smells like her perfume, but it's <u>faint</u>. When I lifted my coin collection album, one of my envelopes fell on the floor. I crouched down to pick it up and my eyes grew wide (like Kakeru Daichi's in the *Ganbare, Kickers!* cartoon) because I realised Anya knows! Anya knows about August 15 because she used to send me money for my birthday every year! I wanted to run into the kitchen and see the cake, but I had to finish my rituals first. Once I had looked at the rest of my prized possessions and put them back in their place, I tucked my chair behind my desk at a 45° angle facing the door (so it looks inviting) and switched off my lamp.

When I entered the kitchen, I found Anya sipping tea at the table. I never drank tea in Germany, but Anya gave it to me one day and now it's what we like to do every morning at 8 o'clock. It's our ritual together. She has a very special machine on the stove that looks like a tall silver pot with a matching (smaller) teapot above it. The first time Mrs Balashova and I had our session in the kitchen, I asked her what it was.

'What do *you* think it is?' she said.

'Hmm… The big pot is for cooking vegetables. That's why it has a spout to drain the soup.'

Mrs Balashova laughed and squeezed my cheek. 'It's called

a *samovar*. We use it to boil water, and the pot on top is for boiling tea.' I liked the sound of that word. I brought out my small blue notebook where I write all my favourite words (Mama had received it as a gift from the bank) and wrote *samovar* in it.

When Anya looked up, she nodded good morning to me with a sugar cube between her teeth. I sat down and drank the tea and ate the pancakes and jam she had placed in front of me. Anya knows to set the table with my favourite spoon and fork (the ones with the holes on the bottom that look like an owl). I looked around the kitchen quickly (to avoid suspicion), but I couldn't see any evidence of the cake. I said *Felix Felix Felix* to be happy, but I couldn't stop the sadness from resting on my face like a bird, a <u>sad</u> bird. Anya must've seen this because she opened her mouth to say something, but then she closed it again. I know I'm a big boy now that it's <u>August 15</u>, but I wanted to cry.

Mama always baked me a carrot cake with extra frosting for my birthday. She'd bring me the cake in bed and sing for me (she had to sing softly because we didn't want to wake up Papa). As soon as she'd finish singing, I'd take a deep breath and pretend to blow out the candle, but she'd interrupt me by singing 'Happy Birthday' in French. And when she'd finish that, I'd take another deep breath, but she'd start singing in English. I'd steal a pinch of the frosting to make her laugh, but she'd only shake her head at me. Mama and I used to act a lot for one another in this way. We were always acting, Mama and me. For example, I didn't really like carrot cake, but I asked for it every year so I could get Mama to explain the carrot story.

This is <u>the carrot story</u>:

Around the time Anya was born, we were fighting the

Allies in a war. The British were clever because they'd blackout their cities at night so our planes couldn't see their targets. But their planes were still able to shoot down our planes, <u>even at night</u>. They had one really good pilot called Cat's Eyes who hit twenty of our planes. But Cat's Eyes had a secret weapon, a special radar, that helped him locate the bombers. The British didn't want us to know about their secret weapon, so they created propaganda (false information) saying pilots like Cat's Eyes ate lots of carrots to help their night vision. And people still believe carrots give them night vision. Ha ha.

After I finished my breakfast, Anya pointed at the clock and said Mrs Balashova's name. She fanned her hands to let me know Mrs Balashova was visiting us at 10 o'clock. We'd already had our weekly session yesterday so it could only mean one of two things:

1. It was an emergency.
2. Mrs Balashova knew about <u>August 15</u>.

I quickly got up and placed my dish and cup in the sink and said *spa-si-ba* (thank you) to Anya. I had around an hour and a half to work on my journal before Mrs Balashova came (she was never late).

When Mrs Balashova saw me, she planted wet kisses on both my cheeks and gave Anya a white box with red ribbons on it. She asked me how I was in Russian and I said *ha-ra-sho* (good). Anya brought Mrs Balashova's tea in the glass cup with the silver holder. Anya had changed her dress into a green one that matched her eyes, like Mama's. She had never changed for Mrs Balashova before. Her lips and cheeks were redder, too. Maybe she had remembered it was August 15?

Mrs Balashova sat down and fanned herself as she wiped the sweat off her forehead. I didn't know why she was drinking tea if she was already sweating. She complained to Anya about something as Anya cut the ribbons and opened the white box. When Mrs Balashova realised I was still standing by the doorway she asked me to *sit, sit, Felix.* 'Do you like honey cake?' she said.

I shook my head.

'What? Never tried a Russian honey cake? You'll be licking your fingers, I tell you.' She pretended to kiss her fingertips.

I smelt the burning candles even before Anya put the cake in front of me. I knew I couldn't wish for what I wanted the most, so I decided to save my wish for later and blew out the candles anyway. Mrs Balashova clapped her hands and said I had become a little man now. She breathed heavily as she lifted her big purse from the floor and fished out two presents. They looked like books (which made me very happy). 'Happy birthday, Felix,' she said. '*Z-dnyom-rozh-deniya.*'

I unwrapped the first one. It was a picture book, and the cover was a boy (about my age) sketching a train.

'This will help you learn Russian,' she said, smiling. 'The boy is a *po-chee-mooch-ka* like you – he asks a lot of questions.'

I turned the pages and saw the boy going on a ferry with his family, then playing ball with his grandmother, then being read to by his mother. I closed the book and smiled with my teeth to show I liked my present, that it didn't make me sad. The second one I opened was a big red book. I knew exactly what it was because Mama had many of these. I turned the pages and put my nose between them so I could smell the old paper (it smelt of damp). I stood up and hugged Mrs Balashova tightly.

'Now, Felix, that dictionary is mine and the only copy I

have. I'm lending it to you for the time being. You'll take good care of it, *da*?'

I nodded. '*Spa-si-ba.*'

When I sat back down, I realised Anya had placed an envelope (no stamp) in front of me. I opened it and saw the Russian money inside. I became shy and only said *spa-si-ba* without hugging her. She gave me a sad bird's smile.

'What a lovely gift!' said Mrs Balashova. Anya was playing with her dress as Mrs Balashova spoke: 'Think of all the wonderful things you can buy for yourself!' She stood up to pass me the knife and once I had cut the cake, she turned it around and cut it into neat little slices for us. 'Anya has allowed me to take you on an adventure today,' said Mrs Balashova, with a mouthful of cake. 'You'll be coming to my house to meet my Vladimir and Valeriya – isn't this delicious?'

I took a bite of the cake and even though it was very tasty, it was no carrot cake, no carrot story. I looked at the big red book that had *Deutsche-Russische* written on it and thought of Mama's dictionaries. Mama translated books into different languages, you see, so she always had a dictionary next to her. I once made the mistake of saying a dictionary was the world's most boring book. But it wasn't a mistake because Mama took off her glasses and looked at me. 'Open it,' she said. 'What do you see?'

'Words,' I said.

'And…?'

'Their meaning.'

'Yes,' said Mama, 'but what about the words?'

'What *about* them?'

'Felix, look at me,' she said, turning in her chair. 'Every combination of letters that has a meaning is in that book you're holding. Which means every story ever written is in there.

Everything that has happened and everything that will ever happen is in that book.'

I looked at the words again, but they made my brain warm. 'So… if I study the dictionary, I'll know the future?'

'No,' said Mama, her face becoming soft. 'But you will understand the power of words.'

'Felix, are you listening?' said Mrs Balashova.

I nodded.

'You can take your presents to your room and get ready while Anya and I have a chat.'

I had just about finished packing when Mrs Balashova knocked on my door (even though it was open).

She laughed. 'We're only going for a couple of hours. There's no need for all that!'

I tried to lift my school bag and realised it was too heavy. But how could I make friends with Vladimir and Valeriya if I didn't have any nice things to show them?

'Come, Felix, we're going to miss the bus.' Mrs Balashova grabbed my hand and walked out of the room. She yelled goodbye to Anya as she opened the front door.

It was hot and sticky outside and seeing people made me dizzy. I could hear them chatting and the children screaming as they ran, but I tried not to look at them. We crossed the street and passed an old man who tipped his cap to Mrs Balashova (she knows everyone).

'Just up this way,' said Mrs Balashova, pushing my hand down as she walked (she has a bad knee). The crickets kept buzzing and the pavement was hot like a barbeque grill, making the air in front of us wavy. Mrs Balashova let go of my hand to pull out her fan. When we arrived at the bus stop, she squinted at me. 'When was the last time you went out, Felix?'

I shrugged.

'But… don't you go to the shop or the park with Anya?'

I felt like I was getting Anya into trouble. 'Oh, yes,' I said, 'I go with Anya.'

'Look at all these nice boys and girls. You need to go out and make friends.'

I raised my head and saw a girl on a bicycle and three boys playing football with a purple plastic ball. One of the boys was wearing a blue Reebok shirt, but when he ran close to me to catch the ball, I realised it said *Reebook* on his shirt.

'School is starting soon,' said Anya, 'so for your homework I need you to make one friend today. It can be anyone you like.' She smiled at me.

I hated it when even Mama made me do that. I didn't need any more friends.

The bus came and Mrs Balashova gave the bus driver some money so we could get on. It was full of people and even though the windows were down, everyone was sweating. Mrs Balashova was holding onto a rail and told me to hold her other hand. When a few people got off, we went further inside the bus. A man stood up to offer his seat to her, so she lifted me by my armpits (which hurt) and put me on her lap. I didn't like sitting on Mrs Balashova's lap because she's <u>old</u>. I tried to lift myself by pushing down on the dirty green handle in front of me so I wouldn't break her. My arms and legs were really hurting by the next stop, and the <u>bad thoughts</u> kept coming to me because I knew my hands were dirty and the germs were spreading. I wanted it to be over.

Mrs Balashova finally tapped me on my bottom to make me stand up so she could pull the cord.

When we got off the bus, I remembered to ask: 'Why do you speak German?'

She smiled. 'My father was German. He brought us back to Russia because my mother missed her family.'

I smiled back at her. Papa sort of did that with me. Except I didn't know I was missing Anya. But I did miss her, especially then.

'Come along, Felix. It's that brown one over there.'

Mrs Balashova lives in a brown and cream apartment that has seven floors. There were four white, three silver, and two black cars parked by the front and many children playing in the courtyard. Mrs Balashova lives on the first floor (which is good because there weren't a lot of steps to climb for her), but there were prams and bicycles in the stairwell, and it smelt like garlic and cheese (which was not very good). When Mrs Balashova unlocked the metal door to let us in, there was another wooden door behind it.

'Felix,' said Mrs Balashova, pulling me back. I really wanted to go to the toilet to wash my hands. 'We must take off our shoes first,' she said.

I looked down at the shoes placed in a neat row in front of me and realised they were all bigger than my feet, so Vladimir and Valeriya were going to be much older than me. This made me sad because I wanted to complete my homework for the day.

'Wear those,' she said, pointing to a pair of pink plastic slippers in front of me.

'Vlad, Lera, come here!'

I turned to Mrs Balashova. 'They speak German?'

'Of course,' she said, walking ahead of me in brown slippers. She stood in the hallway in front of a small table that had candles, a bible, and frames of Jesus, Mary, and Joseph. She made the cross and kissed her hand and then touched the feet of the big white Jesus pinned to a black cross. She lifted a beaded necklace and started playing with it. 'Go have fun, Felix,' she said under her breath.

I bent down and untied my laces.

'Hi, Felix. I'm Vlad.'

I was still on my knee, but I could see his hand, and even though mine was dirty, I shook his. When I was fully straight, I saw how tall he was.

'This is Lera,' he said.

'Hi,' said Lera, stepping forward. I shook her hand as well. Lera wasn't wearing any socks with her slippers, but her toenails weren't painted. I don't mean to be rude, but I didn't think Mrs Balashova's children would be so polite (they didn't even make fun of me for wearing the pink slippers).

'We were just playing a video game,' said Vlad. 'Do you want to play with us?'

'*Da*,' I said. I didn't know they had video games in Russia.

We went into their living room, where there was a small television in a brown cabinet, and a sofa, and dining table. The sofa had a thick plastic cover on it and there were paper mats with flower patterns on top of the wooden furniture. They also had a small balcony where they kept an airer with colourful clothes pegs.

Vlad picked up one of the controllers and gave it to me and then sat on the carpet and crossed his legs. 'Do you know how to play?'

I nodded. My old neighbour, Jakob (he was only five), had a Sega. I hadn't thought about Jakob for a long while.

After I played one round, I turned to Lera on the sofa. She was watching me play with her hand under her chin. I reached out and offered her the controller. 'Don't worry,' said Vlad. 'She doesn't mind watching. Shall we play something together?'

'Okay.'

Vlad took the game out and placed it in a drawer. He picked up another game and blew into it before pressing it into the console. 'Matushka doesn't like it when we play this game' – he restarted the Sega – 'because of all the fighting.'

I didn't know who Matushka was, but I was glad Matushka wasn't there. It was the funnest game I have ever played. I won once out of four times and Vlad said I was very good. When Mrs Balashova came into the room, Vlad quickly switched off the TV.

'Come set the table,' said Mrs Balashova. 'Felix, you can help as well.'

'Yes, Matushka,' said Vlad and Lera at the same time.

Mrs Balashova had cooked so many things. She had also made my favourite: *Olivye* salad (a very delicious potato salad with pickles).

We hadn't finished setting the table when we heard keys rattling in the main door. I listened as the doors were shut and the person took off their shoes. I had just become used to the four of us and didn't want a fifth.

A man came into the room and walked towards Mrs Balashova first and kissed her on the cheek. I had forgotten that Mrs Balashova had a husband. He was taller than Papa and was wearing dark grey socks. I thought Vlad and Lera would run to their papa like in the films, but instead, they shook his hand like businessmen.

'Felix, this is Sergey Balashov,' said Mrs Balashova.

I shook his hand. He didn't smile at me.

When Mr Balashov went into one of the rooms, Vlad and Lera started talking again. We continued to set the table and when Mr Balashov reappeared, everybody became serious again. Before we ate, Lera said a long prayer (in Russian) and afterwards Mr Balashov said *spa-si-ba*. It was the first time he had smiled.

We ate silently. I wasn't enjoying my *Olivye* salad (4.5 for food). Anya's salad is better (Anya puts carrots in hers), but it wasn't only because of that. Mr Balashov made me feel like a statue. When Mrs Balashova said, 'Anya says you love *Olivye*, Felix,' Mr Balashov cleared his throat. So, Mrs Balashova repeated herself, but in Russian.

I nodded and said *spa-si-ba*. Lera smiled at me. Maybe she could be my new friend?

After I had said goodbye to everyone, I waited for Mrs Balashova to put on her shoes. 'What was the beaded necklace on the table there?' I said.

'Always asking questions, *po-chee-mooch-ka*. This one?' She took it off her neck. 'This is a rosary. We use it to count prayers.'

'Why?'

She held one of her shoes in her hand, lifted her right foot and slipped it on. 'It's not actually to keep count,' she said. 'It's so that every time you move each bead across, you think about Jesus's birth, death, and resurrection. You think about His mission.'

'So, it's for remembering?'

'Yes, exactly,' said Mrs Balashova. She put it back on her neck and tucked it under her dress. I made a mental note to write *rosary* in my blue notebook when I got home.

Taking the bus was less scary the second time, but nobody gave Mrs Balashova a seat then. When we got off the bus, we saw a man riding a motorcycle that was pulling a big cart with household things in it. He was riding slowly and would stop every few minutes to take out a megaphone and say things in Russian. Every time he did that, a dog would start barking, which would set off other dogs in the neighbourhood. '*Kho-deb-shchik*,' Mrs Balashova said in my ear. 'He's a salesman. He wants your neighbours to know he buys and sells used pots and pans.'

By the time we got to Anya's house, Mrs Balashova's knees were hurting her, but when Anya opened the door Mrs Balashova didn't go inside to sit. She said something to Anya and blew me a kiss. 'Bye, *po-chee-mooch-ka*,' she said. I waved to her.

Anya had changed out of her green dress and was smiling at me. Not a sad smile, a really happy one. I was happy to see her, too.

The first thing I did when I went into my room was to write *rosary* in my blue notebook. I liked the idea of having something to help me remember. This was my first birthday without Mama. In another eight years, I will have more birthdays without Mama than with her. And in fifteen years, I will have two times more birthdays without Mama than with her. I didn't want to start forgetting Mama. I needed to remember her now and keep remembering her. I went into the kitchen and found the red ribbons in the bin. They were wet with food and tea bits, so I washed them. I put them on my desk to dry and brought out my coin collection album (prized possession #3) from my school bag. I opened the pages to where I had taped the Norwegian and Danish coins. I had collected those coins from all the trips Mama had taken. I peeled the tape off the coins that had holes in them and put them through the ribbon. I only had six coins (with holes in them), but I kept the ribbon long so I could wear it like a necklace. I made a tight knot and wore it around my neck. When I moved coin #1 across, I remembered Mama's face. I thought of her green eyes and her left ear (that sticks out like mine). When I moved coin #2, I remembered Mama's singing (when she washes the dishes and when it's August 15). I remembered Mama's wavy hair with coin #3 and her smooth hands like marbles with coin #4. Coin #5 was to remember her perfume and coin #6 was not about Mama, but Anya, and to remind myself about my own mission: to help Anya leave the house. I tucked the rosary under my white shirt and made my birthday wish.

I unpacked the rest of my school bag and put everything back. I opened the red dictionary to find out how to say *friend* in Russian, but I didn't know how to say it correctly. I took my book into the living room where Anya was knitting. I held it up to her with my finger on the word. She placed her finger on the word and took the book from me. But she couldn't read it, so she held the book away from her face and squinted. '*Drook*,' she said.

'*Drook*?' I said. 'Anya, Felix, *drook*.'

Anya looked at me for a moment, without blinking. I saw that her eyes were shining. I got shy, so she closed the book and gave it back to me. She nodded and gave me a half-smile. 'Anya, Felix, *drook*,' she said.

Happy Mabon

Morgan Davies

Emily leant her head against the car window and stared out at the building, waiting for her father to emerge. Beside her, her brother lurched forward, stretching out his seatbelt again and again, trying to make it lock. Jamie lapped at the stream of mucus working its way down his face as he rocked back and forth. He stopped and stuck his fists out, gripping the handlebars of an imaginary motorbike. Twisting his wrist, he loudly mimicked the revving of an engine. Emily kept her eyes fixed on the glass doors of the office as Jamie's noises grew louder.

'Just wait here for five minutes,' her dad had said. It had been twenty-seven minutes by the clock on the dashboard. Jamie leant over to Emily and screamed his motorbike noise in her ear. She lashed out at him, and he pulled his seatbelt loose and went for her with both fists. She swung around in her seatbelt with her back against the car door and kicked at him with both legs. He was older and stronger, but she knew it hurt him when her kicks landed. A loud knocking nearly broke the glass of the window behind Jamie. Their dad wrenched the door open and leant in close to Jamie who pasted himself against his seat. Emily watched as he jabbed his finger in front of Jamie's face and roared at him. He said he would not finish until the scowl left Jamie's face. Jamie did not change his expression, but he soon looked away. Their dad dumped an armful of files on the passenger seat and slammed his door shut. They were already late for the show, and after Hugh had called that morning, they were forced to pass by the office on their way.

The car wound out of the business park and through the streets of the market town. They drove past the darkened church that had closed earlier that year and waited at the lights by the cenotaph where a group of girls sat on the steps, sharing chips from a bag. Emily looked at her dad's hands as he drove. He wore a battered gold band on one finger, and there were thick squares of hair on each digit that she liked to stroke when he sat next to her on the sofa.

'Dad, can we go the back way?' she asked.

'No, sorry, we're late. Maybe on the way home.'

She liked it when they drove the back road over the mountains. The smooth slopes of the hills folded themselves higher and tighter together there, like the pleats of a curtain. There were lakes like tinfoil in the distance and the dark stain of the forest to the south. When they reached the highest point, and if the day was very clear, she could see the one great, black mountain in the distance.

The clouds mustered overhead as they drove along the main road through the valley, shadowing the course of the railway. Emily tried counting the sheep on the hillside next to her. They entered another long patch of trees, and she gave up and began to play with the ashtray in the door instead. Her dad kept glancing at her and her brother through the rear-view mirror. His eyes lingered longer on her each time.

'Hey, Emily. What's orange and sounds like a parrot?'

'Hmm… don't know.'

'A carrot.' She smiled and the small strip of his eyes and nose grew warm in the rear-view mirror.

'Can we watch all the bike races this time?' Jamie asked him.

'You know the answer to that, Jamie.'

'It depends on my behaviour?'

'Correct.'

'Can we go to the Earth Tent?' Emily asked. The Earth Tent was the one run by the 'hippies' as her dad called them. She loved the handmade clothes that hung in rainbows from the stand and the smooth wood carvings of the old gods of the earth. There was the strange smell of incense blended with the scent of wet trodden grass, and the women who would say 'Happy Mabon!', with coloured stones and silver ringing their fingers, or sprouting in shiny eruptions from their ears and noses.

'What, that hippy place? Yes, you can choose something from there, my sweet.'

When they reached the showground, they joined the queue of cars that stretched along the hedgerow leading to the fields. The tips of the marquees were visible, and Jamie squirmed excitedly at the distant sound of revving engines. A thin-haired steward in a high-vis jacket with a cigarette jutting from his mouth directed them to the far field where the cars and trailers were lined in neat rows. The grass was damp and pungent. Pallets had been laid for the coming rain and after they had parked, the children ran to catch up with the long stride of their father. His eyes were fixed on the open gate ahead, and he carried his clutch of files under a damp armpit. They made their way through the rows of white tents, weaving through the milling crowds. Groups of men in caps clustered together and talked while their dogs stretched on their leads, sniffing out scraps of food that had fallen amongst the trampled grass. A troop of girls walked past giggling and looking behind them, followed by several boys in lumberjack shirts with open collars revealing the thick chains hung around their necks. Their dad led them on a shortcut through the marquees where they leapt over the guy-ropes, past the moaning generators. Loudspeakers pumped out a crackling fog of messages and a wave of humming, bristling air wafted at them as they passed the beer tent. On one stall, mounds of flesh, pink and black were heaped behind a chilled glass counter. Emily stopped and took in the pile of purple liver, the protruding white bones and the tray of kidneys like large and bloody beads. A bald man in a butcher's apron was serving, his bare arms stamped with tattoos like the markings on the pork rind in front of him. He spoke in Welsh to two aged ladies who leant forward and inspected the meat through their glasses. He held a round joint of meat in one hand and pointed to it with the other as he spoke. He turned to Emily.

'Sut gallai helpu ti, blodyn?' Emily froze as the three of them looked at her. She turned and ran, pelting through the crowd until she caught up with her father. When she reached him, she took hold of his hand with its square tufts of hair, and he gave hers a gentle squeeze in return.

They reached the stall of her father's company, a large tent lined with tables which were crammed with display vaccines, disinfectants, milk equipment and other products in gleaming, white plastic. Her dad rushed up to Hugh and began to spread his files out in front of him. Hugh was a short man with a grey and ginger moustache that used to frighten Emily when she was smaller. He glanced at her and Jamie and returned to the files. He was generally gruff and rude, and she did not like him much except for one time after his wife had been ill when he came round with bags stuffed with sweets for her and Jamie. She and her brother ate them while Hugh told their father how sorry he was that their mother had died; he left when Jamie got sick from the sweets.

Hugh and her father pored over the papers together, and the children ran over to feel the metal of the huge machinery outside the opposite stall. They climbed onto one of the trailers. There was a red sticker on its side with large letters saying 'Mammoth' and a mammoth logo.

'Woolly mammoth!' said Jamie. He put his hands in front of his face and stuck two fingers out like tusks. 'Woolly, woolly, woolly!' He waved them at Emily, and she burst into belly laughter. He went on, sliding towards her on his knees. 'Woolly, woolly, woolly!' She screamed until she was breathless. Jamie stopped and laughed with her. It hurt her afterwards when the laughter had died down and she wondered why he couldn't always be like this.

Later in the afternoon, they were tired of the agricultural stalls and sick of their sandwiches, and they followed their father around, complaining. The clouds were dark and swollen above the valley.

'All right, all right,' he said. 'The races are starting soon, and there's too much to do here. You two go and watch, and I'll see you down there. Stay together, and don't get too close.' Jamie was already sprinting away, and Emily started after him, but her father caught her by the shoulder.

'Make sure he's all right.'

'Yes.'

'You know —'

'Yes, Dad, I know. Can I go now?'

He leant in towards her, cupping the back of her hair with his hand and kissing her on the crown of her head.

'Good girl.'

The crowds were building at the racetrack. The riders' names were being called through the loudspeakers, and the rasp of engines tore at the air. Spectators huddled around the edge, families cheering close to the front. Umbrellas were opened as the first rain began to fall, and small children were lifted onto shoulders so they could see. Jamie led Emily towards a large group of men, and they pushed through a gap in the jumble of anoraks and wellies. They pressed against the frayed rope that separated them from the track. The ground had already been churned into a paste. Stacks of tyres hugged the corners of the track, and ghostly blue fumes drifted silently towards the crowds. The bikes wailed past them in a spray of mud and a flash of coloured stickers, and soon the first real race began. Emily pressed her fingers into her ears as the noise became unbearable.

One race gave way to another, and Jamie grew more excited as the riders picked up speed with each lap. Again, and again the packs of bikes ploughed past them, streaking the wet earth. Emily grew tired of the fumes and noise.

'Let's go now.'

'No!'

'Jamie, I want to go! It's too noisy.' He ignored her and she waited until the bikes went past on their final lap of the race.

'Dad will be here now; we need to go and find him.'

'I want to watch one race from the starting line first.'

Emily followed him as he shouldered his way past the other spectators. She struggled to keep up as he jostled and shoved his way through the tight pack of bodies. She called out to him, but he kept going, slipping through a gap in the crowd ahead.

'Jamie! Jamie, wait!' She could no longer see him, and she breathed in little bleats of panic. 'Jamie!' She squeezed between the men. They barked and bellowed above her as the race began in an explosion of sound. She caught a glimpse of Jamie's head in the crowd. He was standing still, staring rigidly ahead, not facing the race. Emily fought her way towards him through the mass of bodies, frantically calling his name. She slipped on the rubber-booted foot of one of the men and crashed into another, her face pressing against his damp, musty coat for a moment before she pushed herself away. She elbowed past another oily green anorak and saw Jamie's eyes wide and strange and staring. She had almost reached him when he fell to the ground.

'Dad!' The call came out of her blood. 'Dad! Dad!' The men close by looked down and backed away. 'Dad! Dad!' she cried desperately as her brother writhed in the mud below, twisting like a landed fish. 'Dad! Dad!'

'Emily?' A small, plump woman in the crowd pulled her close with her arm. 'What's the matter, cariad?'

Back at the car, they cleaned the mud off Jamie as best they could. Mrs Roberts, the plump woman, helped him into his seat and stroked his head. He was whimpering still, as if he had been woken from a fretful sleep. Emily stood by the car as her father thanked Mrs Roberts. His face was pink and moist.

Mrs Roberts was a teacher that visited their school once a week. She was a kind mound of cardigan and skirts who spoke Welsh to them with a glove puppet on her hand. Emily's dad got into the car and called to her. She did not answer. Her throat felt hard and tight. She squeezed her lips together to keep them from quivering. He called to her again and she turned away from the car.

'In you get now, cariad,' Mrs Roberts said. Emily did not move. She touched the corner of her eye with a finger to push back a budding tear. Her father got out of the car and came over to ask her if she would please get in the car.

'You said we could go to the Earth Tent.'

'I know, I know, Emily, but Jamie has to rest now. You know that. I've had to leave Hugh on his own at the stall. I was supposed to be helping him there until six. I've got so much work to do; I don't know how I'm going to do it all. We'll go next time, I promise.'

Something was gathering and hardening inside her. The sound of her own voice calling for him still haunted her ears.

'It's not for another year.'

He grabbed her arm and walked her around the side of the Land Rover parked next to them, out of sight of Mrs Roberts. He spoke through clamped teeth and the veins bulged frightfully at his temple. When he was finished, Emily quavered as she spoke.

'I knew you were lying.'

'Emily! That's enough!' It was her face he was jabbing his finger in front of now.

'You're a bloody liar!'

'Emily Howells, if you don't get in that car now –'

'You big bastard!' She staggered back as the crack came across the side of her face. Her ear rang like a dialling tone, and she felt the stinging heat spreading across her cheek. His hand was still cupped from delivering the blow.

'Get in the car.'

Emily emerged from behind the Land Rover and climbed into the car, putting her seatbelt on with trembling fingers.

The rain finally broke as the car headed back along the valley. It fell heavily, driving the sky into an early twilight. They journeyed in near silence back to their house at the edge of the squeezed-together town. When they were home, Emily waited as her father led Jamie out through the rain and into the house. He squeezed Jamie's shoulders reassuringly, gently guiding him over the step. He came out and started to unload the car, pulling his jacket over his head to stop the rain from running its wet fingers down his neck. Emily ran inside and pulled open the French windows at the back of the house, stepping out onto the patio. She splashed down the garden path and sat down on one of the soaking slabs. Very soon, her clothes were drenched, and her hair hung in lank clumps as the rain lashed at her bare arms. She heard the French windows slide open and her father calling to her through the noise of the rain.

'Emily! Emily!'

Moments later he was standing in the rain at the bottom of the garden in his jacket and boots, pleading with her. She would get a cold, he said, she wouldn't be able to have any ice cream for pudding, she could watch telly with a hot water bottle and blanket if she went inside, she wouldn't be allowed out to play for a whole week. Emily said nothing. She only wiped the rain from her eyelashes. He leant down to scoop her up. She screamed and struggled the moment he touched her. He held her tightly around the chest and began to drag her squirming towards the house, her heels kicking against the wet slabs. He glanced nervously around him. Emily trapped his hand between her teeth and clamped down. It was his turn to scream, and he dropped her onto the hard stone. He went to pick her up, but she was already on her feet, and she landed a hard kick on his shin. From the house to their right came the sound of French windows opening and he slipped quickly back inside the house.

Emily could see her father watching from behind the glass doors, and she returned to her spot sitting in the rain at the bottom of the garden. She faced away from him and folded her legs towards herself, holding her knees in her arms. The cold rain beat against her head and shoulders. She held on to the thought of him watching, but she felt something else inside of her let go and run with the waters down her limbs and hair, along the streams and rivers, outwards and away from him.

Sometimes I dream about a fish

Polly Manning

It was my idea to start up the fishing again.

I hadn't heard from Ray for a while, except a thank you note for the funeral flowers. I went round and knocked one morning. There wasn't an answer, but the door was unlocked so I let myself in. He was in the kitchen looking at the wall. He wasn't doing anything else, just looking at it. I looked too but there wasn't anything to see.

He looked so lonely there at the table with her things all around, the crockery and nice pictures on the walls and what have you. I couldn't take that.

So I said Ray, how about you and me dust off the rods and go fishing down the pier on Sundays? I said 'Sundays' like that so he'd know it'd be there for him every week and he'd have something to look forward to.

We fished together as boys. We cut school and walked out of town along the river, a tin of worms between us. We took turns on who dug the worms out their mother's garden. There was a weedy spot a half mile or so upriver where the Tawe ran wide and clear over the stones. We kept our rods there, tucked behind a broken-down wall. We knotted our school ties round our arms and crawled into the tall grass of the riverbank in case a council man saw us and fined us for not having a licence. We fished and threw rocks at each other and sometimes took sips from a hip flask Ray had slipped from his father. Sometimes we caught a fish but mostly we didn't. I didn't mind that. It was good to lie in the grass with the sun on our faces and listen to the water bubbling.

We stopped fishing as much when I started my apprenticeship and Ray stayed on at school for his A levels. It was hard to find times we could both make it down the river. Then Ray went on to college and got his job at the Council, and we stopped doing it altogether. He met Catherine and they got hitched. The first few years, I'd go round their house for tea. That stopped too, after a while.

Both of us retired a couple years back, and I'd been thinking a bit about those fishing days since Catherine died and how good we'd been as friends, how I hadn't had a friend like that since. Maybe now he'd have more time on his hands. We could start from the beginning. When I saw Ray in the kitchen it was the first thing came in my head. Let's go fishing.

Ray was quiet a while and I thought he might say no. Maybe he was surprised I'd walked in and invited him fishing like that out the blue. Even before the funeral we hadn't seen each other in a while. I'd bump into him from time to time, and we'd always say we'd do something together soon, but we never did. Life just gets in the way sometimes. You can't help that.

If Ray was surprised he didn't say anything about it. He looked me over with confused eyes, like he hadn't noticed me standing there. Then he said, all right.

I mentioned heading down the river. It's a ten-minute walk there for me, maybe twenty for Ray. We only live a couple streets away from each other, but you wouldn't know it looking at our houses. Mine's a little bungalow on the hill, but Ray lives further down in a two-storey painted blue with a lawn out the back. You can see right across the bay to Port

Talbot from the upstairs windows and there's Catherine's roses in the front garden, tangled up now with weeds.

Let's head down the pier, said Ray. I fancy a bit of salt air.

I must have looked put out then cause he said, I'll bring a flask.

It was lovely that first Sunday, the beach long and golden in the sun and the sky blue as cornflowers, and light sparkling on the water. The pier jutted out to sea on the east side of town, a long, tall slab of railings and concrete. Down below was the lock with fishing boats going in and out and boys stripping off their gear on deck. On the other side of the water were the docks and the big grey warehouse with SWANSEA DRY DOCKS painted down the side.

I brought fold-up stools for us to sit on. Soon as we were settled Ray brought out the flask. My heart sank a bit cause it was a big thermos flask with tea in it, but what can you do? I had a cup. It was decent tea.

He was quiet at first and not laughing much at my jokes. I thought that was normal enough with his wife just gone. Besides, Ray was always on the quiet side. His mother mooned after him as a boy, about how *thoughtful* and *sensitive* he was. Girls at school said the same, too. One of them used to slip poems in his lunch box. I never had much time for that. The problem with Ray as I saw it was he thought too much then started thinking his thoughts were very important, more important than real things like his friends and fishing.

I got a bit nervy with him being so quiet and took to counting the boats chugging down on the water, but after a while he looked round and nodded.

Nice day for it, he said.

Aye it's warm for May, I said.

I never think to come down here, he said.

Good spot for fishing, I said. Plenty of room.

It was easy then. Before long we were chatting away just like in the old days. I drank three cups of tea while we talked about school and the things we got up to, the bushes behind the science block where we smoked his mother's Players.

With us getting along so well, after a while I thought about asking Ray why he hadn't been answering the door all the times I'd gone round to knock for him. But then, he'd come fishing. Maybe there wasn't anything to it. I decided to let it be.

We drew in our lines after a while and hooked up the squid I'd brought. Soon as we cast out again it was like a spell came over us. We sat there dreaming with our eyes open. It was nice to be quiet together. Ray was hunched forward on his stool, watching the tip of his rod.

How you been, anyway? Since the funeral, I said.

Ray kept his eyes on the rod. He shrugged.

Fine, he said. Been getting on. The kids came up last month.

Ray has three kids, two boys and a girl.

How's ah, Lucy? I said. She still look like her mam?

Laura, said Ray. She does.

All that gold hair, I said.

Ray grunted.

I was going to ask something else but just then a lady came by with a dog and asked if we'd had any luck. I went to answer but Ray spoke first.

Nothing yet, he said. Hoping for bass but with our luck it'll be dogfish.

I was happy then, cause Ray had said 'our luck' like the both us was one thing. That was how it felt when we were boys, like we were the same person.

The squid had left a bad stink on my fingers. Ray saw me sniffing and threw over a tea towel from his bag. It was yellow and stitched with bees, with little gold threads in their wings.

You sure? I said.

Ray shrugged.

I got a queasy feeling wiping my hands on those bees. I folded the towel careful in the top of my fishing box and covered it with the *Western Mail*.

D'you think—

My rod went off twitching before I could finish. I jumped up and reeled in slow as I could so as the fish wouldn't get away. There's nothing like seeing that tip bouncing in the air. I looked at Ray in the middle of it all and he was smiling, caught up in the excitement of it. I reeled her as far as I could and Ray took the net and looped it under her and together we lifted the fish over the railings.

It was a dogfish. I slipped the hook out her mouth and held her up.

Nice enough, said Ray.

I didn't mind so much it was a dogfish cause it was the first catch. The skin of a dogfish is a nice thing to feel in your hands, like fine sandpaper. I turned her and the light danced off her skin in a thousand places.

Strange they're called dogfish, I said. More like a cat. Pretty round the eyes like a cat.

Ray hummed. He went back to his stool.

I looked at the fish a while, then got down and put my arms through the railings to drop her so it wasn't as far to fall. The sun caught her eye when I held her over the water and something in the black of it made me shudder. The pain of it was a pleasure and I waited for it to come again but it didn't.

She hit the water with a splash of foam. Then the water cleared and she slipped into the dark blue like a knife.

I hooked fresh bait and went back to my stool. I looked over the cover of the *Mail,* a story about the steelworks, but couldn't settle on the words. I felt Ray next to me like an itch. He was staring up at his rod with sharp eyes, licking his lips.

It wasn't long before he got a bite. He sprung up and started reeling, easing up, reeling again, the weight of it twitching in his arms. I thought about getting up to give him a hand but something about the set of his jaw stopped me.

He was doing all right with the rod, but cutting the line in a wide circle like the fish was giving him some trouble. Fishing's like that, it looks like a man is just holding the rod but he can feel things going through it that are troublesome. Ray was frowning with the effort, cursing under his breath. His hands on the rod were white.

Was that a tea towel of Catherine's? I said.

The reel whirred.

I dunno, he said.

Has a nice pattern, I said.

Clickclickclickclickclickclick –

You reckon so?

I wanted to say something more but then he dipped the rod for a hard pull up. Grinning now.

Slow down or you'll lose it, I said.

Ray cleared his throat and spat out the side. He didn't wait for me to get the net. He hauled the fish all the way up on the line and took it in both hands to get it over the railings.

It was a sea bass. As long as my arm and so fat Ray just looked at it and laughed.

Christ, I said.

The shock of it made me get up from the stool. I went to

Ray and touched the fish and we were quiet a moment. The bass opened and closed its mouth.

Can't be far off eight pounds, I said.

Closer to ten, I reckon, said Ray.

We stood there looking at it. When it started twisting in his arms Ray unhooked it and laid it down on the scrap of newspaper we'd put down for the bait. I was surprised when he took the rock from his bag all ready to go.

Too heavy to swing it, he said. I nodded.

He brought the rock down twice. The fish trembled and went still.

It was getting on for midday by then and the pier was getting crowded with people walking their dogs, families perched along the wall eating sandwiches out of tinfoil. Some of the people turned when they saw the fish, mouths hanging open. A couple of boys walked past while Ray was pulling out the guts. I pegged them around twelve or thirteen, one of them with a little fold-out rod in his hand. The one with the rod stopped dead.

That's the biggest fish I ever seen, said the boy.

They stepped closer and I saw that he was a couple years older than the other boy, a big brother maybe. He turned down the corners of his mouth.

You use squid? he said, bending for a close look.

Ray nodded.

Got it fresh from Mainwaring's this morning, I said. The boy didn't look at me when I said that. He was staring at the fish.

Ray waved them closer. He picked up the bass, tilting it this way and that in the light and opening its fins for them to see. I said I'd caught a dogfish earlier and the younger boy said he'd caught one, too.

We gotta tell Dad about this, said the younger boy.

The boy with the rod nodded.

They said thank you to Ray and carried on down the pier, looking back over their shoulders and muttering.

I cast out again while Ray scraped the scales off the bass with the backside of a knife. He cut the flesh into chunks and wrapped them in newspaper, and put them in a plastic bag. He tucked the bag between his feet under the stool.

The pier started to get empty around two o'clock. People were heading into town for their lunches and a few clouds had sailed over from the west. A grey shadow fell on the sea and the surface ran choppy with wind. I pulled up my collar. Me and Ray chatted about what fish were in season, what we would be getting up to that week, that sort of thing. All the while we were talking his hand kept reaching under the stool and touching the bag with the fish in it.

I tried to start up talking about Catherine a few times, ask him if he was sleeping well or eating much, the sort of things you're meant to ask a person. Ray didn't say much, and after a while I stopped asking.

Before long we'd finished the flask and I was getting tired. Around three o'clock I started packing up my things.

Ray looked at me.

You want to call it a day?

I nodded out to sea.

Tide's going out.

We packed up and headed back into town and up the hill, the bag with the fish in it swinging from Ray's hand. When we got to his place he stopped with his hand on the gate.

Thanks for today, Huw, he said. Felt good to get back to it.

I thought maybe he'd give me a piece of the fish, but he didn't. I thought about asking but that made me feel hot all over.

Good to have the company, I said.

We said goodbye and how we'd do it again next Sunday. I set off up the street towards home. Halfway up I looked back and saw, just before the hedge covered him, Ray at the gate watching me go.

Every Sunday after that we fished off the pier.

Most days we caught nothing but dogfish, but as summer went on there was haddock and cod, and one afternoon I landed a turbot. I fried it with butter and lemon and ate it at the table all fancy.

It was nice to sit by the water with the waves sloshing under us and the salt-smell, and kiddies playing on the beach. There were girls in dresses when the sun came out and it was a nice thing to hear them laugh, the sound like bells ringing. With us being there the same time every Sunday, some of the fishermen passing through started to recognise us before long and waved when they went by, and that was a nice thing too.

For a while it was just like the old days. I joked about Ray's being a pencil-pusher and he cracked on about the way I sat on the stool. I was a joiner before my back went crooked. Sometimes I caught him looking at me from the side, or else being quiet with his forehead creased like he was thinking hard on something. That made me nervy. But like I said before, Ray's a thoughtful guy. For all I knew, he was thinking what to have for his supper.

Then one Saturday I called him to change the time we were supposed to meet in the morning and he said, ah sorry, I forgot to mention.

I'll have to give tomorrow a skip, he said.

What's on? I said.

I'm going down Mumbles with some of the old crew, he

said. I guess they heard about me getting back into the fishing and thought I might want to come along.

We're on for next Sunday though, he said.

I closed my eyes, opened them again. His breath on the line was a close, damp thing. It trickled down my neck.

Why you going Mumbles? I said.

It's a good spot, apparently. They head down most weekends.

I waited for him to say something else, but he didn't.

After a while I said, course pal, no worries at all. Enjoy yourself.

Afterwards I put the phone on the table and looked at it. I opened a beer and drank it, and opened another.

That night I couldn't drift off. Every time I closed my eyes and looked into the warm dark I saw myself on the pier alone and all the people walking past asking, had any luck? Had any luck? I hadn't seen Ray's old crew in years and they were nice boys, from his Council days. Maybe after a while of them getting to know me I could go fishing more days than just Sunday.

I got up after a while and went to the kitchen and had another beer. Then I put on my coat.

It was blue-dark outside and raining, the water falling in sparks through the streetlights. I set off up the street and the smells came, the wet tarmac and earth and sweet rot of flowers. That made me think about things all those years ago, when I was so happy and sad and not able to sleep through the night, either.

I wasn't really thinking where I was walking, just putting my feet one in front of the other.

The dark windows of Ray's house were like terrible eyes

watching. I put my hand on the gate and listened. Rain tinkled in the puddles. I stood there looking up at the house and tried to picture Ray asleep. Maybe the bed was too big for him now and he slept in the spare room with the bowl of pot-pourri on the dresser. Maybe he got up in the morning and it was a couple seconds before he remembered, and it was like she'd gone all over again. And he'd go downstairs and make himself eggs with it following him, and whatever else he did that day it would always be following him.

People probably gave him soft, sad looks. The lady in the corner shop, his neighbours, his kids. People checking in on him. I thought about that. Poor Ray. Poor lonely Ray in that house all by himself.

I didn't go through the gate. I reached through the railings and touched one of the roses, and a shower of petals came down. I took one and put it in my pocket.

I touched it there all the way home, like silk between my fingers.

Poor Ray.

The next morning I set off down the hill feeling better about things.

It was a nice morning after the rain, sweet-smelling and the grass sparkling wet. Kids passed by laughing and shouting. A couple of them stepped off the pavement to let me through with my fishing things and I said thank you, boys.

Instead of going out towards the pier I carried on through the middle of town to the bus station. It was early enough that it was still quiet, just me and the pigeons ducking about under the big metal roof. I sat on a bench and waited until the bus pulled in.

The journey was maybe half an hour. I'd packed a flask of

tea, and tried to take a sip from the top but the bus turned a corner and it spilled down my leg. A little girl in her mother's lap watched me dab it off with a tissue and I smiled at her. She turned her face into her mother's neck.

I got off on the main street and walked down to the front. On the other side of the bay was the town and its thousand windows blinking in the morning light. There were a few boats out on the water and I panicked then thinking they had maybe gone out there. But I squinted and it was young men out on the boats.

I set off towards the pier at the far end of the village. Through the cafe and the arcade with the lights and sounds pinging all over, and out onto the promenade. They were right at the tip of the pier spread out between a few benches, chatting and laughing away.

One of them whose name I can't remember turned and saw me first.

Huw, he said.

The others turned then and I saw Ray right at the end. He looked over, then went back to fiddling with his rod.

Room for one more? I said.

No one said anything for a while and then the one that'd said my name looked at Ray and shrugged.

I unpacked my things and set up the rod with a small weight, and cast out right on the corner of the railings cause the rest had taken up the front. I offered round the flask and sandwiches. They said they were all right, they'd eaten already.

The one next to me caught a fish after a while, a small one and not very impressive but anyway I said, lovely one that is. He said, thanks, without looking at me.

Ray hadn't come to say hello so I thought I'd work my way over to him. I chatted down through the line. Most of the boys hadn't caught anything but I made sure to say to them all they had a nice reel or asked where they got their bait.

When I got to Ray he didn't turn around. I said, morning. No answer. He was looking out over the water with his mouth in a tight line.

What you doing here, Huw? he said.

The way he said it I thought maybe he'd seen me outside the house. Something twisted in my stomach then.

Whad'ya mean? I said.

I didn't ask you to come.

I thought it'd be a nice thing, I said.

I wanted to say something else but didn't know what.

Then I noticed the rest of them were dead quiet. Their eyes prickled me, even the ones busy fixing their bait and casting out.

I took a step back and looked at them all, and every time I met their eyes they looked away. It felt then like I was drowning.

What's this? I said.

Ray turned round and his eyes were black.

Just go home, Huw.

He said that so quiet I could cry.

I saw us all at once as boys fishing on the river and throwing rocks, and the things we said to each other we never said to anyone else. His soft boy's hand warm on my shoulder, I took another step back and something crashed over.

Then Ray said something else.

His eyes shone wet and the hate in them came right out and touched me, and I was so afraid.

You had to have her.

It was the way he said it, like I'd done it to spite him. That was never true. In the end I couldn't help it. I tried to help it for a long time. I kept out the way, spent less time with them even though I missed being with Ray. I missed them both.

Then she'd come knocking one night when I was awake and damp with it, just the thought of her turning me inside out.

But that was a long time ago. It was so long ago I can hardly stand it.

After Ray said what he said on the pier, I thought he'd swing for me but he didn't. He just stood there with his eyes shining wet, and that was worse, so I packed up my things. I left.

That was in August. It's November now, and I haven't seen him since. I still don't know how he found out, or when. Maybe she told him, after the sickness wore her down and I hadn't been in touch all those years out of shame. She was an honest person. It's one of the things I liked about her. I don't know what she liked about me. It doesn't matter anymore.

Maybe he already knew that first morning I went round. His hands were folded neat on the table, I remember, like he was expecting someone. Like he wanted to talk. That's all I wanted, too. I s'pose that's why I knocked in the first place. He just needed a friend, and the thing about a friend is you'll kid yourself about a lot of things to keep them around. You'll kid yourself until you can't.

Sometimes I dream about a fish. Me and Ray are at the river and we're children again, leaning out over the water. It's a fish you never quite see, but I see it cause Ray grabs my shoulder and points. The scales flash for a moment in the rippling dark and then it slips deep under, where neither of us can follow.

Sunny Side

Keza O'Neill

A Karen in a red fleece and a visor, with a 'computer says no' haircut, sits alone at a picnic table outside the Downs café. She's the type of person who wears shorts all year. Metal sticks of various lengths and sizes are piled beside her. She's chowing down on a rooftile of a flapjack which is pretending to be healthy. Every few seconds she refolds the plastic over the chewed end of the cake and plonks it down so she can prod at her brick of a phone. She repeats the process three times before noticing you.

'Hullo, you must be Allison,' she says. When she smiles, her gums are baby-pig pink as though she's been using those tablets kids swill their mouths with to check for plaque. She has a yellow HB pencil tucked between her ear and her visor.

'Hi.' You pick up a high-vis orange stick at random. There's a weird fingerless glove dangling from the end. You attempt to shove your hand into it. It's tiny.

'No, no, not like that.' She unwedges herself from the bench. She's a solid unit. Aren't walkers meant to be fit? And she *is* wearing shorts. Horrible khaki ones which end inches above a pair of dimpled knees, fleshy as double chins. She wouldn't be out of place delivering the post.

'They have Velcro. Look.' She peels a tab back on the glove, opening it up, and holds it out to you. Does she think you're five years old? Down the side of the sticks are letters designed to resemble flames: EXCEL. Ha! As if. Picked the wrong ones there. You take a step back.

'Go on,' she says. 'Lucy lefty and righty tighty.' Whatever that shit means. You burrow your hands into your puffer jacket pockets.

'Well, yes. I suppose we should make sure they're the right height first. I'm Shona by the way,' she says.

You puff out your cheeks and release the air. *Pffft*. You scuff your trainer toe in a dry patch of soil.

'… those the sticks, then?' you ask.

'Ye-es.' She wrinkles her nose, then the gummy grin is back. '*Poles*. We say *poles*. Sticks is a teensy bit pejorative … er … negative.'

You know what pejorative means. You think she's a *teensy* bit of a dick. A few years ago, you would have said something snippy. *Got a parcel stuck up your arse?* Or *Send my love to Jess the cat.*

'Uh huh,' you say.

Seven or eight more walkers have turned up by now: old biddies in Patagonia and proper hiking boots. You think about sacking the whole thing off, but it cost you a fiver for an e-scooter from Filton; you might as well stick it out. You don't have to talk to them. Besides, you haven't been up the Downs in yonks and it's a clear day and you can see across to Wales. Anything beats doom-scrolling in front of the telly.

'Are your … er … plimsolls waterproof, Allison? It's quite wet in the long grass.'

Plimsolls? WTF? It's May. And you're on the Clifton Downs, not the north face of the Eiger.

'I've got my trail running shoes in the van if you want to borrow them,' Shona offers. 'They're not as sturdy as boots, but they should be ok for this weather. We look about the same size

… in the foot department anyway. No meat on the rest of you. Not like me.' She slaps a hefty thigh. The smacking sound gives you the ick.

Patronising cow. You're not putting your feet in her sloppy seconds. You'd catch a fungus.

'S'all right,' you say. 'I'll manage, thanks.'

You read about it online, Nordic walking. At eight quid a go, it's cheaper than the pool and it's not as if you have to learn how to do it. Walking with sticks (you know where you can shove your pole, Shona), how hard can it be, right?

Wrong.

The biddies stride out Mo Farah style. There's zero chance any of them is under seventy, but they streak ahead of you. You thought exercise might help with your insomnia. That, and cutting down on caffeine, but at this rate, you'll be adding an extra spoonful to your morning Nescafé to keep up with the blue rinses. You've only been at it ten minutes and you're officially knackered and panting like a pervert. The old dears chat as they walk, paired up in smug little couples. None of them is out of breath.

Shona pauses, waits for you to catch up, chirruping out instructions as the others pass.

'Head towards the bendy trees … left at the ice cream van.'

'Opposite arms and legs, Joan.'

'Looser in the shoulders, Monica.'

'Very nice, Allison, try and get some more traction through your poles. That's it, push down from the strap not the elbow. We'll have you keeping up with the group in no time.'

You stab the pole into the ground, trying not to think about other people's clammy hands inside these gloves before yours. You raise your head and notice a group of twenty-somethings doing Mil-Fit on the playing field to your right. A group leader in commando gear barks orders at a buff girl and three triangle-shaped lads. Yuck. That looks as bad as the gym. You hate the gym. Sweaty, snotty people, breathing gunk over the machines. Grim. Most of them haven't even washed their hands after taking a waz and that's a true statistic. Reddit says guys touch their cocks between twenty-three and thirty times a day. For some it's a calming behaviour, the rest are staking out their dominance. Reddit isn't clear on how to tell which. Either way, seventy-eight percent of them don't wash their hands afterwards. FFS you're stressed now; it doesn't mean you're about to stick your hands down your punani.

Between the early start and a double shift at the pub, you're knackered after work. The flat's looking nasty, you'd love to whizz around with the hoover, but the bloke below goes spare if you vacuum after 9pm. You make do with wiping the surfaces and dump some toilet duck down the loo.

Shankz is vaping one of his 'specials' on the balcony next door. If you can call a one-metre metal crate a balcony. You've put a few pots on yours: geraniums and pansies to brighten the place up; you're attempting chilli peppers too. Your tomatoes flourished, until the seagulls got to them. Bloody scavengers. It's bonkers what people give away on the Nextdoor App, the plants were free, and the sofa was only twenty quid. The stuffing's coming out at the bottom but it's a gorgeous sunflower shade and brightens up the entire flat. All twenty-five square metres of it.

'Hey Allison.' Shankz winks at you and readjusts his tackle. (You called it, Reddit.) Half a dozen empty cans of Stella roll about next to his feet. He's gone over the blue biro on the fronts of his faux-suede slippers. No clue why he writes his name on them – that's how you know how to spell it – but the writing fades over time and he freshens it up every so often. You'd think there was a queue of slipper-wearing muggers lining up to lift the manky things. You've never seen Shankz in real shoes. Come to that, you've never seen him outside the block.

'Wanna drink?' he asks.

'You're ok … thanks though.'

Shankz isn't the worst you've put up with. The family before him: four kids, a Rottie and a turtle (not kidding!) lived in a snarling-screaming-barking loop for five years. You wish Shankz would give the Roadman tracksuits a rest, but fair play, he looked after your plants when you were whacked out with Covid. And most of them survived. He even left you cups of vile milky tea when he shuffled across.

'What's on the menu today, Shankz?'

'Chicken dinner. Wan' some?' He blows a gust of meaty smoke in your direction.

It's one of his less offensive choices. You couldn't open the windows for days when he got into crab's-leg flavoured vape.

'Laters,' you say. 'I need actual food. I could eat a scabby horse.'

You slam a jacket potato in the microwave and stick on the news. One bonus about your flat being pocket-sized is that you can watch telly while you cook. You eat six Jammie Dodgers standing at the kitchen counter.

Opening the fridge to grab cheese and coleslaw, you smile, as you always do, at the two furious-looking tabby cats in festive hats. Your Christmas card from Diellza. It was your only card, so you leave it up all year.

She was lovely, Diellza. She was next door after the Rottweiler family. Her name means sun in Albanian which was spot on. She'd cook massive fry ups – *'Practising my*

English cooking, Allison' – and invited you over to share them. You had brilliant chats squished around her stained, crayoned table, with her solemn-eyed twins spooning baked beans and hotdog sausages into their mouths. You couldn't be arsed with most of the neighbours after Diellza. She's in Bradford now, teaching at the University; Shankz has been a fixture since about 2019.

Through the window you hear him making a phone call.

'You Fu— Twa—!' He greets all his friends the same way. His idea of affection.

You turn the TV volume to max to drown him out.

There's a new woman with the group when you join the walkers on Tuesday. The grannies buzz around her, flies on jam. They never did that with you. You can understand why: she's the flamingo to your pigeon. Her hair is somewhere between blackcurrant and grape with thick lime-cordial streaks. Her sunglasses are mahoosive circles, the size of jam jars, with sea-green frames. The only plausible explanation is that she's been on a beyond-the-grave shopping spree with Dame Edna. She's wearing hiking gear, but she's pulled rainbow-coloured woolly socks over her trousers and painted black and yellow stripes across the toes of her boots, as though she's stepped in giant bumblebees. At first you think she's young, but when she faces you straight on, you realise she's about your age. You're knackered forty. Feeling-it forty. She's a peachy, shiny, big-red-glossy-lips Gwen Stefani forty. Hair in dreadlocks on purpose, not because she hasn't had a hot shower in months. It's hard to feel squeaky clean when you've slept on the streets, even if it was when you were a teen. Something sticks to you. A grimy coating which you can't scrub off.

'I'm Iris,' she says. Her voice is caramel; slow and silky. Because for Iris, people make time to listen.

You don't talk to Iris at the beginning of the walk. Daphne traps her. Monica scurries behind them grasping for crumbs of Daphne's attention. Normally you find Daphne restful. Her full-on opinions don't leave room for questions. It takes the pressure off. But today you can't be arsed with her skewed brand of wokeness. Her easy dividing line between people who deserve her pity and the ones who don't.

You make a great show of being best friends with the B-list grannies, exuding a drunk-aunt-at-a-wedding energy.

'Is that a new fleece, June?' you ask.

'My name's Joan. And I wear the same top every week.'

Joan has thick flaps of skin under her eyes. The colour rises in her cheeks, but the flaps stay white.

'You're lively today, Allison,' says Shona.

You don't smash her stupid visor off her head, although your insides are egging you on. You shrug your shoulders and force your authority-figure smile, refined for use on the social and the fuzz.

'Slept like a baby, didn't I.'

It's morning and the sun hasn't warmed up yet. After a clammy night with the window shut to keep out Shankz's latest – wasabi pea – the fresh air is a relief. You stride out towards Goat Gully and for once you're faster than the group. The view of Avon Gorge should be gorgeous today. Iris catches up with you as you pass the Travellers' camp.

'Phew. This is harder than I thought it would be.' She looks straight at you when she talks and she's pretty enough to make you catch your breath.

About fifteen caravans are parked along the Ladies Mile.

There's a clothes horse outside one, with laundry drying; rows of kids' T-shirts and an odd number of towelling socks. A cluster of primary school-aged girls kick a tennis ball between them. Iris jerks her head behind her.

'Who are they?'

'Travellers' camp. They park up here most years. Don't mention them to that lot, you'll unleash hellfire. NOT IN MY BACK YARD!'

'As in—' She glances towards Daphne, crosses her eyes and sticks out her tongue, then flicks her gorgeous green-eyed gaze back to focus on you.

'Got it in one. The wrath of Daph.'

She laughs and her eyes crinkle up at the corners. Her eyelashes are full-on Jessica Rabbit.

'Where are you from, Allison?'

'Been around.'

Do I detect a *tipyn bach* of *Cymraeg*?'

Three things hit you simultaneously.

She's Welsh.

You recognise her.

This was bound to happen. You've been waiting for it. The law of averages says you had to bump into someone from Aber at some point. But if you'd listed a thousand names, you wouldn't have guessed who the person would be.

Walking Iris. Lovely Iris … is Iris Whittaker, from school.

You consider changing your walking day, but there's no sign she recognises you.

You don't let yourself think about Aber. It's a rule. You don't go there. Or dwell on the years between then and now. Before this flat, before your *fixed abode*; a phrase which stuck when you didn't have one.

In those years you drank whatever you could get your hands on. You did what you needed to do to get by. Newport. Cardiff. On to Bristol. You slept on the steps outside the old Lloyds bank building on Harbourside. Some nights you stayed in a shelter in St Paul's, some you didn't.

When you moved in, you made a pact with yourself not to look back. No regrets. No guilt. You'd live in the moment. You bought a lined exercise book from Spar. You tore out a page and wrote down all your sad thoughts and the names of everyone you'd left behind. You folded the paper in half again and again and again until you couldn't fold it anymore and then you put it in your mouth and chewed. It took a third of a bottle of vodka to wash it down. You wanted to puke, but you choked it back. You haven't so much as sniffed any booze since then.

After six weeks, you've worked out how to flick the poles off the straps (not gloves – chill pill, Shona) without taking one of the biddies' eyes out. On walking days, you sleep through the night; and you're down to three ciggies a day. Wonders may never cease. You look forward to walking. You look forward to seeing Iris.

The Travellers have moved on, but Daphne's latest meltdown is about plans to relocate Bristol Zoo to Cribbs Causeway.

'Another community asset under threat,' she says. 'I never thought this day would come … We Bristolians have cherished our zoo for one hundred and eighty-six years. Green spaces, historic buildings, libraries … toppling like skittles and nothing done to prevent it.'

'Like skittles,' sighs Monica. 'Bristol Zoo's a hallowed ground. I've always th—'

'Piffle, Monica. There's no point in thinking … Action is

what we need. Action! Think of the poor creatures. Parcelled up, shunted about, no idea where they're going, some sent abroad, away from everything that's familiar … And what about the unwanted animals, the unpopular ones? Euthanised, no doubt.'

Funny, when the conversation was about wood-burning stoves, Daphne forgot her green credentials. Everything was about homeowners' rights.

Daphne pauses mid-stride to unclip her straps. She blows her nose loudly on a large, monographed hankie. Monica blinks as though trying to stop tears.

'Don't upset yourself, Monica. I'm sure the new place will look after the dear animals,' says Joan. 'The *Post* shared details of the new enclosures they're building at the Wild Place. There's going to be a central African forest area for the gorilla troop. Won't that be wonderful for Jock and his family?'

'Poppycock! I'll believe it when I see it. I've already signed the petition to have this tomfoolery stopped. There are plenty of places they can build flats,' says Daphne.

You want to lay it on Daphne that there are nineteen thousand families on the waiting list for affordable housing in Bristol, but you don't. This lot are so blooming clueless, they think shopping at Lidl is living on the edge. The things Daphne comes out with. She'd have sent Mother Teresa loop-de-loop, sticking her fingers in her ears and screaming at the top of her lungs.

'Perhaps they could put some of the people from the housing list in Jock's new enclosure?' suggests Iris. 'Room for at least thirty asylum seekers, I should think.'

Iris drags you to the pub. She moved from Wales at Easter.

'C'mon. Please, Allison. I haven't got anyone else to go with. Pretty pleeeeze.'

Her cheeks are round and appley and she's wearing tonsil-pink lipstick today. Shiny and gloopy. You imagine scraping a jammy slick off with your finger and smearing it over your own lips.

She works in a nursery, but her passion is photography. She shoots landscapes, but she prefers underwater. She goes scuba diving, but snorkelling's better. Snorkelling is a safari, in the sea. There are barrel fish and wrasse, dolphins and porpoises and oh, the jellyfish. You should see the jellyfish.

She swings on her chair until the front legs come off the ground, then scoops a handful of Scampi Fries into her palm from the open bag on the table. She crunches through the crisps without pausing. She's not afraid you'll hear her chewing.

'I'm sorry, Allison. Look at me blabbing on. I've barely asked you anything about yourself … If I'm not spilling my guts, I'm feeding my face. My sister says I've got an oral fixation.'

As she realises what she's said, a raspberry pink blush spreads across her cheeks. With her rainbow hair, flushed face and sparkly green eye shadow, she makes you think of a Care Bear. You nibble the centre of your bottom lip and wind a length of hair around your finger. You're glad you let the bleach grow out.

'I'd rather listen than talk,' you say. 'But I am partial to oral.'

You head outside to wait for the bus and Iris stumbles against you. She's broader and heavier than you are, but she's been on the Jack and Coke, and she's gone floppy. You loop your arm around her shoulders to stop her from falling, propping her against a brick wall so you can support her weight. She gets the wrong idea and slides down the wall and onto her bum. Her tights are laddered, and she must've scraped her arse to ribbons.

You plop down beside her, and you want everything but you're afraid of wanting it, so you run your finger over the creamy skin on the inside of her wrist where the pale blue veins peep through. Iris leans in to kiss you and you catch a waft of orange, beeswax and Scampi Fries. You scoot closer. For an instant, the world fades away and you hear unicorn hoofbeats, angels with harps and tweety birds singing. Moonbeams and sunbeams and all that cartoon, corny shit; but Iris misses and lands a smacker on the fleshy part at the bottom of your ear. Your earlobe is covered in her gloopy, sticky, wonderful lipstick. You both crease up. She whinnies a horsey laugh, snuffling and *bruh huh huh huh.* Her bonkers guffawing makes you both giddier.

'Allison?' she whispers when she stops braying.

You don't answer. You can't, you're still laughing.

'Allison?'

You close your eyes, try to calm yourself, control the tickle at the corner of your mouth.

Iris shuffles closer and wriggles a bit until her face is tucked inside the curve of your neck. She's bigger, but she fits. As though she is the missing piece in your jigsaw. She laps the lipstick from your lobe with dainty, kittenish flicks and then she sticks the point of her tongue right inside your ear. It's squelchy. And now it's you who is falling.

Iris's photos are insane. She says they're taken underwater, but you see aliens from outer space. You had no idea that it was so colourful underneath the sea. There's one you can't stop staring at.

'What is it?'

'*Pysgod wibli wobli.*'

You understand what she means, but you pretend you

121

don't. You don't tell her that it's not proper Welsh anyway and the real word is actually *sglefren fôr*.

'It's a jellyfish,' she says.

There were shedloads of them on Aber beach every summer. Compasses and Mauve Stingers and Lion's Manes. Dried and dead and crusty, or gross and gelatinous. Iris's jellyfish is luminous. Like her. A fuchsia mushroom-cloud explosion with streams of strawberry ribbons stretching behind it. Reflected on the creature's surface is an iridescent rainbow.

'How did you—? The light—?' You struggle to find the words.

Iris tucks a strand of hair behind your left ear, the one she kissed.

'You have to take it from the sunny side,' she says.

Monica's celebrating her quincentenary. Five-hundred walks, not five-hundred years. Granted, it might have felt that way listening to Daphne. She's sporting a new hairdo for the occasion, pale pink and foamy as though she's emerged from a bubble bath. Standing next to Iris they could be from the same family of colourful sea animals.

Shona wants a photo for the website. You duck behind Daphne and Iris.

'Squidge together! That's it. After three. *Nor-dic walking.*'

Iris tries to catch your eye on the 'dic'; normally you'd be in stitches at this coming out of Shona's mouth (oops, my bad, Shona) but you're trying to dodge out of shot.

'Allison, I can't see you. Little ones at the front, please,' says Shona.

You retreat further.

'She gets self-conscious in pictures.' Iris drops her pole to squeeze your hand, the Velcro on her strap sticks itself to yours. You squeeze back.

You're spooning in bed. Iris is snuggled inside you, your hand cups the curve of her breast.

'Allie,' she murmurs. 'Allie.'

You stiffen. You feel as though the rectangle of folded paper which you swallowed has worked its way back up to your throat.

'How long have you known?'

She turns in towards you and tries to take your face in her palms, but you won't let her.

'How long?'

'I won't say anything,' she says.

You tug on your jeans and hoodie without showering and scramble around looking for bits of your crap that you've dumped at her place. Even after four months you didn't trust yourself to leave more than a worn toothbrush and a spare pair of pants.

'Allison. Stop. Don't.'

You don't stop. You rummage on the floor for your socks, banging your head against the foot of the sofa. The carpet is scuzzy. You dust bits of lint off your clothes, not that they're anything special.

'I don't understand. Don't you want to go home?'

You shake your head.

'Your parents were broken when you left. For God's sake, Allison, everyone thinks you're dead. Your sister –'

'No.' You scrape your hair into a ponytail, pulling it tight enough to hurt.

'Did something bad happen? You can tell me. You can tell me anything.'

123

'No.'

'No, you won't tell me or no, nothing happened?'

'Just no.'

'Then … why? I don't understand.'

She tries to hold you; you shake her off. You fold your arms against your chest and look past her pleading eyes at the jellyfish photo. There's a miniscule seahorse silhouetted in the bottom left-hand corner of the frame that you hadn't noticed before. You wish you were lying pressed up against Iris listening to her silky voice explaining how she captured them both in the same image. You wish you could hug her and walk everything back.

'It's too late,' you say.

'For what?'

'For everything. All of it. This.'

You pull your zip right to your chin and lift the hood over your head. You close the door softly behind you. Iris is crying.

'I won't tell anyone,' you hear faintly through the door.

Iris WhatsApp's you:

Hope u r ok. 😿

I walk on Mon now. U can change back 2 Tues if u want? Or another day.

I love you Allison. I'll stop messaging now but I'm here when u r ready.

Local TV Bristol shows a retrospective about the Zoo. Most of the hour is taken up with the history of Wendy the elephant. They talk about the BBC series *Animal Magic* which made Wendy a celebrity. You loved that programme when you were little. The presenter, Johnny Morris, made up funny voices for the animals. You fought voice-battles with your sister trying to—

You mute the sound until the *Animal Magic* segment has finished.

When you turn the volume up, the presenter is explaining that Clifton residents often used to stand in their doorways watching zookeepers escorting Wendy down Whiteladies Road to the BBC buildings. You know Daphne will – *would* – have something to say about that. (Because *of course* Daphne lives in Clifton.) Doubtless Daphne galloped through Bristol on Wendy while doing a tango in a fur bikini, or something else extraordinary. You'll never get to hear, whatever it was. You pick at a piece of dry skin at the side of your thumbnail. You'd kill for a ciggie.

When Wendy arrived at Bristol Zoo, her name was Georgina, but they changed it. At first she shared her enclosure with a companion, Christina, but Christina got sick and had to be put down. Wendy wouldn't settle with another elephant after that. She lived alone for sixteen years, until she was euthanised in 2002.

You work at the loose skin with your index fingernail. It will hurt if you keep at it, but you do it anyway.

You phone Iris and half-wail-half-mumble out Wendy and Christina's story. Iris listens to your squelchy sobbing. You can't tell if she understands what you are saying, but she keeps repeating 'It's all right, Allison. It's going to be all right.'

When you are spent and breathless and hiccupy, Iris waits. You listen to her regular, even breathing. She stays on the phone until you hang up.

You hear Shankz blundering around on his balcony-cage. You stick your head out to tell him to keep it down.

'Allison!' He's sweaty and looks half-cut. 'Come and have a drink wiv me.' He holds up a litre bottle of vodka.

You come up with this wild idea about surprising Iris at the Nursery and taking her swimming. Your cossie sags around the bum, but it's the thought that counts, right? You dump the stolen orange and beeswax shampoo (sorry, Iris) over your head and lather until your hair is as big and foamy as Monica's quincentenary 'do'. You shave your underarms and legs and make a hatchet job of your bikini line. You sniff. Gross, booze is seeping out of your pores. You scrub everywhere, making your chest and arms red, but you can't wash it away. Your tongue is thick and coated and three Nurofen haven't taken the edge off.

You stick your fingers down your throat and retch into the toilet bowl until only stringy green bile comes up.

It's not enough. You get off the bus twice to spew.

Paper cut-outs of rainbows, shaded in scribbly wax crayon, decorate the nursery windows. Some are traditional ROYGBIV, some are freestyle with magenta, Smurf-turquoise, dog-turd brown or salmon pink. Those ones are mega. You imagine Iris crouching down to help a bunch of pre-schoolers with their masterpieces. Her focused gaze, the pink tip of her tongue peeping out between her shiny lips. The undecorated windows have one-way mirror glass so you can't look through to find her. Reflected back at you is a dull-complexioned woman with hard, tired eyes. She looks scuzzy, frightening, a woman who might do something terrible to a child, and you know you can't go in.

There's a kiosk shop at the sports centre. They sell plastic snorkels and masks. You blow half a week's shopping money on an acid-green one.

Babies in bright inflatables splash at the shallow end. A fat toddler in dragon water wings chortles as his mum dunks him in the pool. A deflated beach ball and a jumble of foam floats lie discarded behind the lifeguard. You sit on the edge of the pool and dip your feet and ankles in the water.

Beneath the clamour of voices, the pool's filtration system provides a murmur of white noise. You fix your mask in place, take a deep breath and go.

You let in the thought which has been your constant companion, pushing, pressing, hurting, wanting. The dream which slips into the pit of your stomach when you least expect it, slithers upwards and puts its hands around your throat. There, submerged beneath the water, blowing gentle bubbles, you let it come. *Home,* you think. *I can go home.* And you imagine Iris, her Ribena hair swishing around her face. You see a jellyfish, who lives life on the sunny side, and you know where home is.

The Stopping Train

Jo Verity

Jim Casey spends the first few days getting over jet lag and avoiding his London agent. Conrad finally pins him down and, over a champagne lunch, they celebrate the success of Jim's latest novel. Over the years, his books have done well enough – a couple made it to the big screen – but topping the NYT chart bumps him up into a different league.

Naturally, with success comes expectation and, by the time the waiter brings coffee, Conrad is sniffing around. 'So, what have you got for us next?'

Jim winks and taps the side of his nose in, what he hopes, is a reassuring gesture. Truth be told, for the first time in his career, he has nothing. But he's contracted to deliver a first draft by Christmas and he dare not let on.

The first stop on his tour is the Book Nook in Canterbury. Par for the course, two thirds of his audience are middle-aged women kitted out in crumpled linen, looped scarves and dangly earrings. He tells them a bit about himself. Gives a reading. Takes questions. When that's done, he signs using the Waterman his ex-wife gave him for his seventieth.

Then he's off, zigzagging from town to town, from bookshop to library to literary festival. He's in excellent shape and he needs to be as his schedule is taxing. But he's not going to complain. His publisher has stumped up for first-class travel and booked him into the kind of quirky hotels Americans tend to go for. This spell away from his desk may be the very thing he needs to kick-start his creativity.

He's the only passenger in a first-class carriage, somewhere between the last place and the next, when the train slows to a halt in a shallow valley.

On either side, fields rise up to woodland. The sky is a soft, washed-out blue. Ragged hedgerows are capped with flushes of dog roses. Swallows skim a meadow shimmering with buttercups. Butterflies fidget from blossom to blossom. Brown-and-white cows stand in the shade of an oak tree, swinging their heads and flicking their tails. Halfway down the field to his right, a sheep – or maybe a calf – lies sleeping in the sun.

As he looks out of the window, it comes to him – he'd be happy to die. *Here*, in this idyllic meadow on a perfect summer's day.

He's felt this kind of certainty before – a long, long time ago.

He's packed in his vacation job with Dagenham Parks Department, 'borrowed' ten quid from his mother and he's standing in a lay-by on the outskirts of Morpeth, thumbing a lift to Edinburgh. An articulated lorry draws to a halt on the opposite side of the road, stops for a moment or two then pulls away, leaving behind a girl and an enormous rucksack. The girl is small and dark-haired – a slip of a thing in a yellow dress – and as she looks across at him, she smiles. And he knows.

By the time he gets off the train, he has the makings of a plan. He's due to head home after tomorrow's gig but something happened back there. Something meaningful. Magical. Mysterious. So, here's what he'll do. He'll reschedule his flight, hire a car and go take a look at that field. A few more days will make no odds.

His last engagement goes smoothly. Why wouldn't it? He's had plenty of practice. Although there are times when he'd welcome a heckler to pep things up, or a tricky question to prompt an in-depth discussion. Once in a while, that happens – but not today.

Back at the hotel, he noodles around on his iPad, dragging the little man onto the map, twizzling him around, searching for his valley. Of course, Google mappers travel in cars not trains but when he switches to 'aerial view', he still can't find it.

He makes a 'to do' list. Contact the airline. Call Conrad. Book a couple more nights at the hotel. Hire a car. To be honest, he's excited at the prospect of going off-piste. A tad nervous, too. It's quite some time since he's had to make his own travel arrangements and technology has made it more challenging. He's heard horror stories from friends who've managed to check the wrong box and arrived at the airport to find they're not on the passenger list.

And then there's Ethan. Should he let him know there's been a change of plan? Probably not. He's aware of this trip but not the fine detail. He checks his watch. Colorado is seven hours behind which would make it late morning in Denver. He pictures his son, blond and lanky like his mother, standing in front of a class, doing his best to persuade them Henry James is relevant to their twenty-first-century lives. He was disappointed when Ethan opted to teach high school. He'd hoped the boy would go for something less pedestrian but he's forty-two now with a timid wife, three kids and an overdeveloped sense of duty.

Setting his phone to charge, he brushes his teeth, gets into bed and mulls it over. Maybe he should forget this whimsical nonsense. Stick to his original schedule. And yet. *Something* went on when he was on that train. He closes his eyes and, lulled by the murmur of voices in the room above, attempts to retrieve that sensation.

Instead, he's back in the lay-by.

The girl in the yellow dress is still there and, without giving it a second thought, he crosses the road. She's not what's considered beautiful but her face, her whole being, radiates energy. When she smiles at him, thundering juggernauts and stinking diesel fumes vanish.

'Where are you heading?' he says.

'Away from that fucking festival.' She has a Scottish accent and crooked teeth.

With that, his compass swings from north to south, Edinburgh abandoned for wherever she's going.

'Jimmy,' he says, holding out his hand.

'Lily.' Her hand is soft and warm, a tiny creature resting in his.

'What's in here?' he says as he hoists her rucksack on his back.

'My worldly goods.'

Next morning, Jim strolls along to the train station. En route, he stops by the bookshop and buys an OS map of the area which he's pretty sure includes his field.

The woman on the desk at the station is cheerful and patient but she struggles with the fact his enquiry has nothing to do with tickets or timetables. Obviously she knows the stations his train passed through but she can tell him nothing regarding the terrain between them. He's not deterred. If anything, this spurs him on. Quests are, by definition, challenging.

Over the last few days, the temperature has soared and he stops at 'Gwyther – Gentlemen's Outfitter', where he treats himself to a Panama hat, a late (and pricey) birthday present to himself. He's the only customer in the shop and the guy who serves him seems happy to chat.

'Perhaps you can help me,' he says, spreading his map on the counter. 'On my way here, my train passed through some picturesque countryside. One particular valley caught my eye.' (He doesn't mention it being a nice place to die – that would be downright foolish.) 'Peaceful. Unspoilt. Woodland running down to fields. Any ideas?'

It transpires the man is not only a hat aficionado but he also has extensive knowledge of the locale. 'Ahhh. That'd be...' he circles an area with his forefinger, 'hereabouts. You're right, it's a beautiful spot.'

Encouraged by his confidence, Jim returns to the hotel and sets about changing his flight.

The hire car turns up mid-morning. It's a VW, half the size of his SUV but perfect for the task in hand. These winding roads demand concentration and, turns out, the route he's chosen is barely more than a lane. It takes a while to acclimatise to the stick shift and he finds driving whilst navigating somewhat tricky. In places, foliage obscures the road signs and before long he's not sure where he is. But it's a glorious day and he pootles along, taking in the scenery, glad not to be standing in line at Terminal Three.

Settling into the ride, he turns on the radio, switching channels until he finds Radio 3. In an instant, the car is filled with rolling hills and chasing clouds, thatched roofs and apple orchards. Elgar gets him every time and, eyes welling, he pulls into a field entrance and switches off the engine.

Lily plays classical piano. She speaks Italian and can identify birds from their song. She gets edgy if she hears a father shout at a child. When they go to the pictures it doesn't take much to make her cry. They've made a pact not to trawl the past but it doesn't stop him wondering.

They wander south and west, finding work along the way, ending up at a caravan park outside Falmouth, helping in the farm shop and keeping the plots tidy.

When October winds send the last holidaymakers scurrying home, they move into town. He gets a job with a painter and decorator whilst Lily gives Italian lessons to anyone who'll pay.

He loves the quiet domesticity of their life but he knows she will soon tire of it.

When the music finishes, Jim blows his nose and resumes his journey.

A couple of miles on, he spots a pub set back from the road, and a hankering for a long, cool pint lures him into the car park. His is the only vehicle in sight but it's a working day in an out-of-the-way place so perhaps it's not so surprising.

The pub door is propped open with a log, and he ducks to avoid whacking his head on the door frame. It's blessedly cool inside. Tiny windows set in thick walls allow little light to penetrate and it takes time for his eyes to adjust. When they do, he sees dark furniture. Skull-cracking beams. Worn flagstones. A proper, old-fashioned rural pub.

'Hello?' he calls. 'Anyone at home?'

Lowering himself into the shabby armchair by the stone fireplace, he studies the room more closely. Empty glasses on the bar. Winter coats on hooks by the door, incongruous on this sweltering day. He listens. No murmur of voices. No clatter of pans. The place is more Marie Celeste than the convivial hostelry he'd anticipated. All the same, it's a relief to be out of the sun, and leaning his head back, he inhales the fragrance of beer and tar from the blackened chimney.

They spend the winter evenings in the pub, sitting close to the fire, eking out a couple of pints.

'I need the sun,' she says one night when they're in bed, twined round each other for warmth. 'Let's go to Greece.'

'What'll we use for cash?' he says.

She pinches his thigh – a vicious, heartfelt pinch.

'Hey,' he says, 'what's that for?'

'For being so boring.'

They have no money for tickets, and his passport is in his bedroom at home. But this is a test and he's not about to fail due to practicalities.

'Greece sounds good,' he says.

She runs her hand across his belly and kisses him, long and hard, her teeth nipping his tongue.

When they get off the overnight coach, he needs to pick up his passport.

'Come and meet my parents,' he says.

She shakes her head. 'I don't do family.'

They arrange to meet at Victoria in time for the boat-train. But when he gets home, he discovers that, two days ago, his father suffered a stroke. His mother can't stop crying. She clings on to him, saying his turning up out of the blue like this is a miracle.

He meets Lily as planned and explains the situation. 'Dad's dying. I can't walk out on them now.'

'And I can't hang around.' Her voice is tender yet firm.

'Write to me when you find a place,' he says.

She nods and blows him a kiss. 'Take care, Jimmy Casey.'

When he wakes, he gives it one last try. 'Hello? Where the hell is everyone?'

Losing patience, he helps himself to a bottle of water from behind the bar, gulping it down, the ice-cold liquid jangling his teeth. Pulling a five-pound note from his wallet, he places it next to the till and, as he takes a second bottle, he gets the feeling he's being watched. He swings round, expecting to catch the voyeur but, of course, he's alone.

A couple of miles further on, he reaches the place Hat-man pinpointed. Spotting a finger-post, he pulls off the road onto a grass verge, the rutted soil suggesting he's not the first to stop here. The sign points over a stile towards a footpath leading into a wood and, grabbing his hat off the passenger seat, he locks the car and climbs over the stile.

Here and there, roots break the surface of the well-worn path and he needs to watch where he puts his feet. Sunlight strobes through leaves, spattering him with dancing shadows. He smells bracken and fungi. Hears whizzing insects and a robin trilling.

After a few hundred yards, the footpath veers to the left, holding the contour, but his sense of direction tells him to keep straight on. Once off the path, the going gets tougher, the spongy ground booby-trapped with rabbit holes and fallen branches, all concealed under a carpet of leaves. He edges warily down the incline, turning his feet sideways-on to improve his stability. Brambles snag his trousers and snare his ankles. A low branch flicks his hat off, another scrams his cheek. When he goes to clean it up, he realises his bottle of water is in the car.

He's beginning to think he's got it wrong, when the trees thin out and his spirits lift. Hat-man was right. There, beyond a single strand of barbed wire, lies his valley.

Hoisting the wire, he ducks under it and sets off down the hill. The gradient is steeper than he bargains for and he braces his knees to stop himself careering to the bottom. (*Young Jimmy would have launched himself down the slope, arms spread wide, whooping for joy.*) Halfway down, the ground levels off forming a plateau before resuming its canter down to the train tracks. This plateau offers an ideal vantage point and flopping down, he shucks off his shoes. Catching a stalk of grass between thumb and finger, he strips the head, tossing the papery seeds into the air.

Well, here he is.

Taking a few deep breaths, he surveys his surroundings. The field across the valley is dotted with sheep. A pair of crows are on lookout in the topmost branches of the oak. A not unpleasant smell of dung hangs in the air, although today the cows are nowhere to be seen. A smudged contrail is the only blemish on a blue, blue sky. It's as perfect as he knew it would be.

The scramble through the wood has taken it out of him and he lies down, shifting his hips until he finds the comfiest spot. The crushed grass beneath him releases its timeless scent. A bee returns, time and again, to a clump of clover, its drone soporific.

The sun is fierce and, covering his face with his hat, he shuts his eyes.

He's back from the States, clearing his mother's house when he comes across Lily's postcard at the back of a drawer. The picture shows an island set in a cobalt sea. When he flips it over, her message tells him all he needs to know. 'Tholos Taverna, Anafi. I'll wait here for you.' But the tragedy is, it's come seven years too late.

The card weighs nothing, yet he knows the weight it carries will

scupper him and, downing the remains of his mother's bottle of
brandy, he summons up his courage.

    With sheets of newspaper from the scuttle, he creates a pyre in the
grate and balances the postcard on top of it. A couple of flicks of his
Zippo, and the job's done. It hurts like hell but he has no choice if he
wants the world he's making for himself to keep turning.

When he comes to, his hat is wedged under his hip. Hat-man
would not be impressed and as he sits coaxing the whisper-
thin straw into shape, his thoughts begin to settle.

    It's been a weird couple of weeks – especially the last few days.
He'd counted on this time-out to spark ideas or, as Conrad would
put it, 'move things forward'. Instead, he's been lured down the
rabbit hole of what might have been. Truth is, every life lived is –
always will be – predicated on 'sliding doors' moments. Pointless
indulging in what ifs and if onlys. Decide whether you're in or
out, then make it work. It's the only way to stay sane.

    A distant thrumming invades his meditation and,
simultaneously, a chill wind picks up, sweeping across the
meadow, swirling the grass and raising the hairs on the back
of his neck.

    The thrumming grows more insistent, and as he gets to his
feet, the train noses out from a coppice of hazels and, brakes
sighing, grinds to a stop.

    Silence and stillness descend on the valley and, crazy
though it is, he knows the train is waiting while he chooses
what will happen next.

    Shoving his feet in his shoes, he starts scrambling up the
field. Once or twice, he trips and goes down on all fours. His
thigh muscles are soon screaming and he's tempted to pause
for breath but he keeps going, and only when he's on the other
side of the wire does he stop and look back.

Sure enough, those cows are back under the oak. Swallows are swooping. Butterflies, fluttering. Across the valley, sheep are playing follow-the-leader.

And the train? It's on the move again, meandering up the track towards its next stop.

The Boys on the Bridge

Brennig Davies

JANUARY

Your end is a beginning

January first The wee small hours

Pull up to the bridge in a silver Toyota Aygo you saved up for when you were seventeen Kill the engine We watch you sit behind the wheel for a bit, like you're steeling yourself We think back to when it was us, in the cars we saved up for when we were seventeen, driving to the bridge and then just sitting

Elsewhere, all the people you love sleep, or sing 'Auld Lang Syne', arms wrapped around each other A few text you You can't bear to read the messages Throw your phone over the side to obliterate on the rocks, then get swallowed by the swollen river

At the beginning, we watch you climb awkwardly onto the railings, shaking like a man who's ferried himself to the scaffold Fireworks still going All the dogs in all the houses, quivering on the sofas We try to grab you, but we can't

Try to tell you not to, but you can't hear, and we're not meant to do that, meant to just stand and watch

So we watch you step off the bridge and get obliterated, below, on the rocks

Watch you swallowed by the swollen river

FEBRUARY

The funerals are always tough

What's fortunate is that you miss yours, because your paperwork doesn't come through in time, and as your mourners shuffle into the pews you're still stuck in Limbo

We go, though We float in and hang in the vestibule

This town is used to funerals by now It's had to get good at them, its skills for grieving honed by practice like the whetting of a blade So many of us dying, in such quick succession – no wonder people know how to play their parts so well

The aunties and uncles Your Year Six teacher, Miss Finney Your cousins, young men like you Your friends, none of whom are holding it together Our friends were the same at our funerals

Your kind-of-but-not-really girlfriend wears a black dress and heels and doesn't know what to do with her hands, aware that she knows no one, if that's possible in such a small town, or at least knows no one *well,* at best your friends who slagged her off when you fought but are too busy now, wrapped in their own grief, to bring her into the fold

And then your mum and dad, who both look dazed and exhausted, vaguely disbelieving, like they've just gone twelve rounds but the bell keeps ringing for more Your dad is practically carrying your mum, who is like a sack of bones No one's left to carry your dad

But it's your younger brother who looks the worst He trails a few paces behind them, looking obliterated The puppy fat has dropped off him In its stead, a wrecked man's leanness His eyes are as red as if someone has poured salt into his sockets

We've seen that look before We've been there No good comes of it

We watch all this from the back of the church Think of our brothers and mothers and half-girlfriends The same vicar who did our services does yours He knows exactly what to say, which beats to hit and when

Has the whole practice down to a fine art

MARCH

The first flowers of the year are starting to come through when your paperwork clears, and you join us

You look confused Ask, where am I?, though you know it's a silly question

You know where this is Last time you were on this bridge you were leaping off it

Things look different in daylight They always do

Where are the pearly gates?, you say, Saint Peter?, but none of us really believe in all that, whatever the priests preach And if it's true, well, we've not seen it yet

Welcome to the gang, we say And we are a gang by now, properly There's at least ten of us now, us dead boys on the bridge, and now you're here to join us

I know you, you say, staring into our faces We went to the same school You were two years above me And you, I saw you in the papers I saw your mother in the chip shop shortly after you jumped Even when her chips were swimming, she couldn't stop pouring the vinegar

Yep, we say, for we speak in one voice now Soon you'll speak in our voice too That's us

Your face changes, like a cloud passing through the wide, scoured-light March sky My mum, I've gotta go see her Tell her I'm okay

You can see her, we say, but not talk to her She won't hear you

You say, I've changed my mind I don't want to be dead anymore Who do I speak to about not being dead anymore?

It's funny and it's not, so we laugh and then we don't

We forgot how young you were How young you'll always be

No, no, we say, soft-breeze-gently That's not how this works

APRIL

For the whole of April you're in denial

You spend the lengthening days hunting for a portal, a loophole you might thread yourself back through It starts off sad and quickly becomes annoying

You're not getting back, we say

You try and literally dig through the dirt on the ground

Look around, we say You jumped off this bridge, like we all did Now you have to live with that

We acknowledge the words' irony and move on

Why are we all still here then?, you say

Fair point Why do we linger like a bad smell? Why, even after we've died, are we doomed to never leave our hometown? We can float anywhere we like, as long as it's within this town's limits We can't go any further than this, than the docks and the waterfront Their dark, grey, dark-grey dishwasher waters The newsagents, where we bought our fags and Twixes, the playing fields behind the school All that empty space

I'm not like you, you say I don't want to be like you

At Easter you get it into your head that if Jesus came back, so can you

You were never the brightest

You float down from the bridge again, down to the rocks and the river Kneel on the banks Grab a palmful of gravel On your forehead, draw in ash a crucifix

You don't even believe in all that, we say

You tell us to fuck off

By the river where your body washed up months ago, you pray hard for that body returned All those cremated bits reconstructed, flying out from the urn on your parents' mantelpiece and reforming on the carpet in your shape

You pray and pray

New flowers bloom

Cardiff lose 2-0 to Leeds

And through all that praying you remain a shiver, lone and see-through

Slowly, you wipe off the forehead ash and stand up again

I can't believe that this is it, you say quietly I thought that there would be more to death than this I thought it would be different

You die again, a second time, and again we are here with you

This time you can see us The dead-end we're all in

MAY

In May there is a football match in your honour

The town gathers in the stands and claps as the players, some of your former teammates, run out onto the pitch Put their arms over each other's shoulders as they stand, in a line, facing the stands, for the minute's silence The folks in the stands link together too Stare, silently, back Everyone thinks of you, and of us, though some people struggle to remember our names now

So it goes C'est la vie One day it will happen to you

The referee blows his whistle and the match is struck, the sky a scraped colour

The boys play well

We can see that you're itching to join them You can't stop following the ball with your eyes like some panting border collie

When one of your former best mates scores a goal, you float up high into the air, somersaulting, yowling with glee

When you float back down, we look at each other, then look at you

Go on, we say If you want to, join them

You look at us, surprised, like you didn't think this was allowed

It's not But we nod anyway

After half-time, you float down to the pitch and join your teammates And because we're all linked together, joined by an eternal invisible chain, we float down too They cannot see us at all Even to each other we're just a shimmer, shoulder to shoulder with all this flesh and blood But when the whistle goes, we run with the rest of them, whizzing across the mud and green When the ball reaches your foot it passes right through it Same with other players who, when we're in the way, run right through us and shudder Doesn't matter We're having so much fun So much fun

At the end of the game, people get upset again They hold each other and clap At the clubhouse they drink pints from plastic cups and say, He'd have loved that

And you say, though only we can hear, I did

And your best mate, who organised the whole thing, stands up on a chair, thanks everyone for coming, says, There were times there where I actually felt his presence, like, like he was still with us

And you nod, though no one can see you Only we hear you say, I was

JUNE

It's your birthday in June

We don't normally bother to mark birthdays though you still have one, technically, a date stamped on all your documents, your passport to The Next Place, but what's the point celebrating once the clock's stopped? The candles always glow the same number

Someone celebrates for you, though

We float over to your house to find your brother with a cake

Chocolate, with white stars on it We think he must have made it himself

We can't eat anymore, but we still remember how these things taste The sweetness, the moist texture, the way it would sometimes stick to your teeth

Your brother is on his own now, with your cake

He cannot see us all there with him, spectres at the feast

He lights no candles He sits and eats the whole thing, and does not move until he is finished

The moon is round and white and owls are hooting in the trees, the warm dark We watch your brother vomit into the toilet bowl, over and over, until he glistens with sweat, sounding like a skriking owl, before he lets the warm dark take him

JULY

We watch her arrive at the restaurant

It's not one of the ones to which you took her

She wears a dress with trainers and a cardigan *Radiant* might have been the word if you'd been a poet, but you were like us when on Earth, never too good with words, never too sure of them

We watch as your girlfriend-who-wasn't-really-necessarily-your-girlfriend gets seated and orders a glass of white wine Outside all day it's been sizzling and the night holds on to some of that

The man arrives He wears a black shirt, white jeans, and a gold chain which makes us all roll our eyes But he's gracious, and kind to her, his face open and handsome They talk, these living people, the quick

You keep waiting for her to mention you but she doesn't

Why would she?, we say Why talk about her ex-boyfriend who committed suicide on a first date? And you concede that that's fair, but there's a flare of anger in you still, a glowing jealousy

In that moment, you do what you're not meant to do, what we've all been expressly told is forbidden

You drop yourself into her head, like a drip from a tap into a pail

We try and stop you but we can't

It's one of the first things you're told in the post-death induction You do not enter the living in this way It's dangerous, too high a risk, and often they can't handle it, even if they think they can, even if they think it's a comfort

We are meant to observe, not to participate

And the threat was held over us Break the rules, the last thread that ties you to the mortal coil is cut You're moved on We don't know where to No one who's gone has been able to come back and tell us Perhaps that's also against the rules Probably it is

But you drop into her head, and because we are a pack, we boys of the bridge, we're all dragged in after you

It's a strange, rushing sensation, to be sealed, so suddenly, in someone else's brain

Immediately, we feel just how nervous she is, the jitters, all aquiver though she keeps herself still But there's more

She has a migraine, with all this new pressure in her head But apart from that, through her eyes we look into the face of the man opposite her, and we feel that warm old tug of attraction, hooked through scales and white meat That funny butterfly feeling All frantic but soft as silk She is thinking of you She is thinking how it was like this

with you

And we tug on each other's sleeves, say, We have to go, we have to go, but we can't pull you away, and deep down none of us want to leave, really, because it feels so good to remember To feel a pulse quicken, to feel, with her fingertips, the fine cloth of a napkin, to walk out of the restaurant with this man, wandering through the town like a real creature in the world, a thing of substance, back to his place, and you want to make sure that she's safe, you say it's to make sure that she's okay, to know that it's okay, what is about to happen, that you're pleased for her She brushes her fingers against her temple Like she can feel you, and all the rest of us, in there

Really, when it comes down to it, we should leave

It's perverse to stay Invasive, and unfair

We should all let ourselves out of her head, closing the door quietly behind us, but dammit, we don't

When the touching starts, it feels better than we can ever recall it feeling We linger longer than we should, just to have that rush again, that communion joy

When she throws her head back and cries out, in ecstasy

and grief, a maelstrom of both, we feel it all too, fierce and blinding and huge

It's not a little death at all It's a swell of life-force, of energy, a taste of lightning It is too much Too Much

It makes sense, why this isn't allowed When we finally leave her head, it's unbearable to leave that Too Muchness behind

But it was worth it, we will say that Whatever the price, it was worth it

We leave her, then, and float far away in shame

But we imagine that she must have known that you were there with her, in that moment, and we imagine her smiling, and then weeping when the time came and she realised that you were gone for good, out of her life

We imagine, in the hot summer night, that the man next to her in the bed who is breathing, blood-full, living, held her and stroked her hair and told her, as you'd told her, that one day everything would be fine, and they both got to live in that feeling, that feeling was allowed to be theirs

AUGUST

Inquiries are made Higher Up

Questions are asked, and we stammer as we supply them It seems very likely that this is it, that we will be exiled *Elsewhere*, but then somehow there is a reprieve

This is your first and final warning, the Supervisors say in officious tones *If it happens again…* The sentence hanging like a blade

We miss nearly the whole month of August The mown lawns and wild grass, heavy afternoons, kids on scooters impatient for they're not sure what

We are back in time for A Level Results Day Teenagers

clutching brown paper envelopes, leaping in photos for the local paper

Your brother just about drags himself out of bed to collect the paper with the letters which spell his future They might as well say E N D The words *extenuating circumstances* fall hopefully from teachers' mouths onto the school hall's linoleum floor, but we know that expression well, the one on his face We've been there

He knows he's fucked it

You say, Can't I drop into his head? Tell him it's okay? And we shake our heads like, *Are you crazy?*

He drags himself home, sweating in the grey, sunless heat Climbs back into bed Doesn't cry

Thinks of you and faces the wall

SEPTEMBER

The leaves fall, the way they always do, the way they kind of have to

As the year starts to fade into September, it refuses to go quietly New activity quickens up The rumble of school buses, a feeling of Back To Work New diaries and binders The apprentices walk over the bridge with their new bags, trying to make their faces look older, more capable, than at this point they are This was some of us once, before we decided we couldn't bear any of it

And the other eighteen-year-olds make their pilgrimages to Dunelm and Ikea, become laden with kitchenware they'll begrudge sharing, writing out passive aggressive notes to flatmates saying *Please wash up after yourselves* ☺ *xx* They eat meatballs with their parents It's a new grief every time, staring at these meatballs

And when it's time for the young to leave, the car grows fat with boxes and duvets and clothes horses and houseplants, guitars to pluck at parties to impress people not yet met And when it's all lugged up to a tiny room with a single bed, the eighteen-year-olds make a go of their new lives, in their new, tiny rooms They try to kill off all they don't want to carry forward, heading off in the night, headfirst, into cities they don't know, stumbling down the streets with people who might come to mean more to them than they can imagine now, queuing in the cold by the kebab van, wondering what to choose

But this was never us

People like us don't know this way, don't do things like this, especially not us dead boys

We spend September, as ever, on the bridge

Your brother stays, too, a bird with its wings pinioned He spends more and more time on the bridge with us, though he can't see us

He's planning something You can't see it, but the rest of us can

As the leaves fall, his gaze is trained down at the water, deep into the water, and his gaze does not break

OCTOBER

Hallowe'en is our Christmas

Small kids dress as vampires, witches, white sheets with eyeholes

We get to come back, even if not fully nor forever

It just all gets more permeable, all of a sudden For one night, a brick wall becomes more like a thin net curtain We go home to our mothers, who are still sitting up at the kitchen table, waiting for us They can't see us, but they know we're there

Ieuan, they say, Sean, Sam, Kyle, Lewis, Harry, Jack, Morgan, Joe, Evan, Finley, Andrew, Josh

A litany of dead boys The names go on and on

Why did you do it? our mothers wail Why did you have to do it?

We don't know anymore

Because we felt we had to

All other doors closed

Because what else could we have done?

Cored like apples from the inside, the sadness like a pit from which we couldn't crawl, so it had us, and we went lower and lower, a lift down a shaft

And we had lovers who hated us, babies we hadn't wanted, albatrosses round our necks, and it's all just a fancy way of saying that we were fucked, and there was nothing for us, what should have been the blank pages of our lives already blotted, marred by scribbles, too many livid black marks

And all our friends were dying, and all those boys we hardly knew at the time And the sun was heavy and the sky heavier, and we had no money nor hope

What we'd had of both we'd spent

And we couldn't say these things to you when we were living because you had your own things, your own burdens, and a man does not offload onto others, he holds what he has to carry until he sinks into the ground and the ground closes around him like a zip

Because we have one life, and we did ours wrong And better to end it than to drag others down

Because the town itself was a fist, and we weren't fast enough to run before it closed on us

Because we had cars, and legs, and could carry ourselves to the bridge by the river on the outskirts, the town's limits, as far as we could get

Because we could leap off that bridge and have it all end, the shit, all of it

Because we didn't know at the time that that would hardly work, and what we'd left, we'd miss

And our mothers sit there at the kitchen tables, crying as we whisper through the net curtain, and then some kids knock at the door, dressed up, excited, kids with everything still ahead of them, and they call, *Trick or Treat!*, while our mothers extend their hands out to them with offerings of sweets

And then, when the kids have gone again, our mothers come back through to the kitchens and find no one there, just a chill at the back door, and by morning the wall's back up again

NOVEMBER

They've sold your house

They couldn't bear it any longer apparently, your family Everything in boxes Fed into the back of a removal van, like sacrifices to some unappeasable god

You stand on the short paved drive, facing the house, its doors and windows and clasps This is where I grew up, you say As if this still counts for something Perhaps it does

Your mother and father gut the home, their insides removed as they do it It takes a few hours Winter weans the sun off the sky Your mother and father, once the house is a ghost, get into the van, and so does your brother He carries a box of your things

I have to talk to him, you say Have to talk to him

152

We refuse to let you We're frightened We don't know what happens if you do We don't want to find out

As the van drives away, your brother looks back at what they're leaving, eyes flashing like he's watching something burn And then he faces front at last, silent and still, as if newly turned into a fine-grained pillar of salt

DECEMBER / JANUARY

And then, at last, Christmas comes, your first without a body, and we see that it makes you sad but it's gone just as soon as it arrives

Your brother does not partake in the celebrations He curls up into himself to write notes in his boyish scrawl, when he begins to quietly bid things goodbye

We know the score, the pattern

You know it too, despite your pretence

He walks in your year-long shadow He moves in the ghosts of your motions

This town's wrung the fight out of him, too

The day before the anniversary of your death

when the year itself dies

your parents wilt away beneath covers, hiding their faces, and your brother escapes, slinks out like a shade

It is familiar, and horrible He dresses in best clothes for the mirror, stares into it blankly for a beat too long Grabs the car keys from the sideboard It's further to drive from their new house to the bridge, but he manages

On New Year's Eve the roads stay fairly clear The pubs already soaked with drinkers, streets lined by nightclub queues with girls wearing too little

The countdown's already begun

Fireworks paint the sky all manner of colours, and your brother pulls up where you pulled up not too long ago, in the silver Toyota Aygo he inherited from you

And we can feel it all again, all of us How desperate it is How achingly, nibblingly lonely It's too much, Too Much, but we know it

He gets out of the car It's freezing cold You try to grab him by the collar of his coat but your hands pass through him the way water slides slick over rocks

Don't do this, you shout You'll regret it You'll wish you hadn't

As if he can hear you

Elsewhere, far, far away, people are singing 'Auld Lang Syne', their arms around each other

One day this will be you, you try in vain to tell your brother, who's oblivious

Things won't always be how they are now The missing won't hurt so badly You'll find a wife, or a husband, and love them You could be someone who has children I see you as someone who'd have children

He walks over to the bridge, your brother The chill's in his bones now What good's a coat?

He strips it off, like any figure at the bank of a body of water, preparing to swim

You're screaming at him, your brother, and we're watching you scream, and we can't do anything anymore, dead as long as we have been, but feel sorry for and envious of those who held on

But the year's not worn you down

God, you're so bad at being a dead man

All death's done is made you want to live

We see in your face what you'll do before you do it Like a dive or a freefall, there's too much inertia to stop it

So we watch, as your brother climbs on top of the bridge, and you pour us all into his head, the exact way in which we're not supposed to

And he's staggered by the rush of it Staggers a bit, but luckily does not fall

Jake? he says

You say, Ewan

Where have you been? he says I've missed you Who are all these other people?

So you tell him, you rake it all up The waiting rooms, the light-filled hallways, the never-ending corridors Us, the other dead boys you've met The things you've seen Playing in the football match The heavy-hot summer The cataclysm of grief Hallowe'en The loss of the house

Why didn't you say? Ewan says

You say, I'm not allowed They'll do me for this

And then you say: But I had to say, don't do this You might think you want to, like it's the only thing left to do, but it isn't

And you tell him all there is to live for, all that the dead mourn

Sunshine soaking into skin A glass of orange juice Yorkshire puddings Sex The kind of rib-rattling laughter you only get when you love, very deeply, the one who's made you laugh The fine mist that weaves between the trees of a forest when the weather's cool Music, any and all of it Videos of animals doing incongruous things they shouldn't be doing End of play on a Friday afternoon Nights out Fireworks

You go on and on and on and, as you do, your brother looks up to the sky

Then he shakes his head Bends his legs

Hops off the edge

Back down to the sweet, sweet ground

And the rocks go hungry The rushing water too

We watch like a chorus as you make us all linger in your younger brother's head as long as you can, as long as you can push it, before the Supervisors appear from wherever they appear from and drag us from it, kicking Oh boys, they say, oh boys, you know what this means, and we do We are preparing to vanish for good this time, though God knows where Just not here We might actually get to leave this town

After everything, we'll miss it more than we can say

But not your brother: your brother gets to stay

He steps back from the bridge, his brain suddenly drained of your presence, but still echoing with it, like a call down a well, a call to say,

Help's coming Help's coming

He weeps with the weight of it, all of it, everything, the way we wish we could weep, with the sting and rawness of still living

It's a new year The fireworks are still going There are texts on his phone he will answer

He gets back in the car and drives from the bridge The night offers him a road, which he takes,

with thanks

The door to the Next Place opens and the Supervisors usher us through it solemnly

But just before we go, for a moment longer, we stand on the bridge, we boys of the bridge, and look down at the river, up at the stars, the many thousands of constellations All the bodies burning out and blazing Persisting in the dark

Our end is a beginning

It could be so, it might be so Our end could be just

a beginning

Postmodernity and its malcontents: reflections on the Welsh independence referendum of 2007

Corresponding author: [Redacted]

Key-words: post-truth, referendum, factuality, Wales, Senedd

> *"You cannot live in the present,*
> *At least not in Wales"*[1]

In recent years there has been much wailing and gnashing of teeth over the apparent decline of honesty in public life, heralding the dawn of the "post-truth era". In much the same way that Captain Renault was shocked to learn that gambling was taking place at Rick's Bar, many commentators have been appalled to discover that politicians sometimes adopt a creative approach to truth-telling. Needless to say, none of this is new to students of political science. The manipulation of information is a practice as old as politics itself: from Caesar's *De Bello Gallico* to David Cameron's shed-begotten memoir, the

---

[1] R.S. Thomas, 'Welsh Landscape'.

idea of "controlling the narrative" has a long and rarely distinguished history. Some authors still insist that Machiavelli can tell us all we need to know about political strategy, although frankly such clichés are best left to the airport bookshop, or indeed some of the less imaginative rap singers.[2]

Nevertheless, it would be churlish to deny that the internet age has thrown up new and sometimes surprising means of twisting facts to suit all manner of purposes. Debord gave us society as spectacle,[3] Evans introduced us to the idea of constructed reality,[4] and Surkov has succeeded in transforming politics into the theatre of the absurd. Meanwhile, the kaleidoscopically-fragmented state of online discourse has opened up exciting new horizons for conspiracy theorists and associated dimwits. In this respect the attacks of 11 September 2001 may be seen as representing a symbolic turning point. The proliferation of internet conspiracies has made "9/11" more than just a lightning rod for idiots and oddballs; it has become something akin to a maypole, a virtual space where they can congregate and celebrate the sacred communal rites of idiocy, clucking and gurning like mud-flecked peasants on a mead binge. The millions swept up in this phenomenon have in common a vivid imagination and a stubborn indifference to empirical evidence, underpinned by the conviction that nothing is truly as it seems. Given the sheer tedium of so many modern lives, this is perhaps a case of wishful thinking more than anything else. Nonetheless, the oxygen that social media

---

[2] Readers with an unhealthy appetite for banalities of this ilk are referred to John Etheridge's recent tome *The Art of Strategy*, which contains little else.

[3] Guy Debord, *La Société du Spectacle*.

[4] Eleri Evans, *Damcaniaeth Adeiledd Cymdeithasol*.

have provided to endless (and endlessly tedious) conspiracy theories must surely rank among the most nefarious consequences of the world wide web.[5]

Notwithstanding the calamitous implications for the quality of political debate, and indeed for democracy in general, the distortion of reality has provided fertile ground for research of a psycho-social nature. It is not my intention here to summarise, nor to add to, the sizeable corpus of academic literature which has sprung up around conspiracy theories and their proponents. Perhaps there is indeed something to be learned from a rigorous study of online blathering about voting machines, or Bill Gates poisoning Covid vaccines, or whatever nonsense the Russians are currently promoting. Alternatively, I would argue, there is no shame in deciding that one has better things to do than study the paranoid ramblings of delusional Americans and their manipulators in the international intelligence community.

Much more interesting, I would contend, are those events that truly occur but somehow fail to register in the collective consciousness.[6] One could cite any number of examples, but a few recent instances should suffice. In January 2020, Ukraine International Airlines Flight 752 was shot down near Tehran by trigger-happy elements of the Islamic Revolutionary Guard. News media all over the world grimly predicted a military escalation, but within a few months the affair had been almost entirely forgotten by all but the families of the deceased. More recently, in

---

[5] Along with the explosion in both state and corporate surveillance, and of course the use of "influencer" as a noun, let alone a job description.

[6] Events which do not ascend to the realm of "political facts", as Jacques Ellul would have it – cf. *L'Illusion Politique*.

September 2022, a group of disgruntled army officers overturned the government of Burkina Faso. Those with no more than a passing interest in such events may have experienced a sense of déjà vu: rightly so, since the government they overturned had itself seized power in a military coup some eight months previously. For those who like to keep count, there were no fewer than four successful military coups in Africa in 2021.[7]

It would be tempting to ascribe Western ignorance of these events to our general lack of interest in other parts of the world, or, more generously, to our preoccupation with the Covid-19 pandemic and its aftermath. But there is a virtually endless supply of similar examples from different eras and different parts of the world, all of which should compel us to explore the fundamental questions implicit in our ignorance: What makes a historical fact? Who gets to decide? And what happens when an event is simply too far-reaching to be comfortably incorporated into the prevailing narrative?

The purpose of the present article is to address one particular event which represents, to my mind at least, the most intriguing and enduring example of a phenomenon which was simply too extraordinary for the general public to accept and assimilate. An event of such magnitude, and with such profound ramifications, that a whole society was unable, or unwilling, to come to terms with it. The event in question is the Welsh independence referendum of 2007.

---

[7] For a useful summary of the events leading up to the current crisis in Burkina Faso see S. Hearne's *Exile on Bassawarga Street*. On a purely anecdotal level, it is interesting to note that S. Hearne was married to J. Etheridge from 2003 until around 2015, during which time she published nothing of worth. Coincidentally (or not), her contributions have been much more insightful and compelling since the divorce.

For readers not well-versed in the politics of the United Kingdom, some context may be of service.[8] By 2007, devolved government in Wales was an established reality. Nevertheless, the idea of Welsh politics remained a faintly exotic and entirely uninteresting prospect for almost everybody residing east of Offa's Dyke (and a fair proportion of those on the westward side). Even now the First Minister of Wales can walk down any high street in England without being recognised, a degree of anonymity which is one of the perks of a prime seat in the devolved legislature.

At the risk of vastly understating the matter, in the summer of 2007 Wales was not at the forefront of the UK's political conversation. Tony Blair had finally decided (more or less of his own volition) to make way for Gordon Brown as Prime Minister, and those political journalists not yet on holiday were busy speculating about the possibility of a snap election. For Wales, this meant more of the neglect and indifference to which we as a nation have become accustomed. Despite holding 34 of Wales's parliamentary seats, the Labour Party in London and the Labour Party in Cardiff continued to coexist somewhat uneasily. Blair had reaffirmed his thorough disinterest in Welsh politics by appointing Peter Hain as Welsh Secretary, a post that Hain ostensibly retained even as he devoted all of his time to grappling with the manifold dysfunctions of the Northern Ireland Assembly.

---

[8] Within the limited confines of this article I am unable to explore the broader historical context of Welsh independence movements, but readers looking for a useful introduction to this subject could do worse than seek out Idris Sloper's *Chwyldro Cymru*.

And yet, although Westminster paid little heed, the Welsh political sphere was a veritable cauldron of intrigue in this period. The Assembly elections of May 2007 had seen Plaid Cymru gain seats at Labour's expense, chiselling away the governing party's majority to the point where some form of coalition was inevitable. Despite undergoing heart surgery in July, First Minister Rhodri Morgan was determined to lead the negotiations in person. Buoyed by those recent election gains, Plaid leader Ieuan Wyn Jones was gleefully briefing journalists about the extravagant conditions his party would impose in return for propping up a minority Labour government in Cardiff. Somewhere near the top of that list was a demand for a referendum on full independence for Wales. By his own subsequent admission, not even Wyn Jones himself believed that this was either a realistic or a desirable prospect.[9] Nevertheless, an independence referendum had been part of the Plaid manifesto for so long that they no longer thought to question it.

Fatefully, it was this relic of the nationalists' more anarchic past that inspired what Morgan believed would be his political masterstroke. Determined to maintain the upper hand over Plaid, Morgan decided to call their bluff: he would give them their referendum, it would prove to be an utter fiasco, and the independence "debate" would be settled for a generation at least. He promptly called a press conference and, without notifying either Plaid or his Labour colleagues in advance, announced that a referendum would be held to decide the

---

[9] Contrary to the assertions made by a semi-anonymous reviewer of my recent book *Police and Polis, a radical history*. Perhaps if the mysterious "JE" were not so busy drinking cheap wine and chasing graduate students he might have found the time to actually read the book, and perhaps even understand some of it.

question: "I agree that Wales should be an independent country."

Morgan's intuition was that the nationalists would be woefully unprepared for a campaign on this scale, and that decades of burning holiday cottages and spray-painting *Cofiwch Dryweryn* on railway bridges would prove to be no substitute for actual political experience. As a veteran of the 1997 devolution campaign, and of course the outright victor of the 2003 Assembly election, Morgan knew a thing or two about voter apathy. In private he was utterly convinced that turnout would never meet the required 50%; the whole affair would be a damp squib, and Wyn Jones would be sent scuttling back to Anglesey with his tail between his legs.[10] So confident was Morgan in this strategy that he set the date of the referendum for Thursday 13th September, paving the way for a triumphant appearance at the Millennium Stadium for the Wales – Australia Rugby World Cup tie on Saturday 15th, and a follow-up celebration to coincide with the tenth anniversary of the devolution referendum on September 18th.

With the benefit of hindsight, Morgan's calculations now appear hopelessly naïve. But in July 2007, nobody could have predicted that the people of Wales would be even remotely interested in an independence referendum. The Senedd elections had been and gone without much fuss, and once again the voting public had showed no great inclination for

---

[10] One small obstacle to Morgan's referendum gambit was that he had neglected to consult Gordon Brown in advance. Brown was suitably furious, primarily because he had other plans and absolutely no intention of wasting his time on Welsh politics, but the First Minister succeeded in winning him over. For a first-hand account of their (somewhat animated) discussions see Z. Williams, *Caerdydd/Llundain.*

Welsh politics. For weeks on end the country's biggest talking point was whether or not Shambo the sacred bull should be put down to avoid the spread of bovine tuberculosis.[11] Morgan's strategy was predicated on the widely held assumption that most Welsh people were tacitly opposed to independence, and thus no real campaign was required. Of course events would soon prove otherwise, and the summer of 2007 did not provide the rest and relaxation that Rhodri Morgan's doctors had advised.

Morgan's surprise announcement left Welsh Labour in an uncomfortable position. A clear majority of Assembly members were opposed to leaving the union, but campaigning against independence for the country you purport to lead does appear to suggest a certain lack of both confidence and competence. Morgan decided that the best available option was to allow AMs to vote "with their conscience", with the expectation that senior Labour figures would weigh in to the debate at crucial moments in support of a "No" vote.

Meanwhile, the forces of opposition were gathering in a small office above a bookmaker's shop on Cardiff's Westgate Street. Launched with a budget that would make a shoestring seem enviably robust, the Yes Cymru campaign was led by a curious assortment of doughty Plaid veterans and enthusiastic student volunteers. The latter provided some eye-catching ideas for attracting voters who might usually have given Welsh politics a wide berth: Yes! branded condoms, rowdy club nights, and of course a flurry of online activity centred upon Facebook. Their efforts were greatly supplemented by a raft of celebrity

---

[11] There was to be no happy ending for poor Shambo, alas.

endorsements, ranging from Eddie Butler and Shane Williams to Bryn Terfel, Rhys Ifans, Charlotte Church and two-thirds of the Manic Street Preachers.[12] The Yes movement also benefited from the support of some more seasoned political campaigners. By now free of the constraints of the Labour party, Ron Davies relished the opportunity to further the cause of devolution. His speeches at rallies in former coal-mining communities were particularly well-received.

Caught off guard by the unexpected dynamism of the independentists, a No campaign had to be hastily assembled. This proved to be far more difficult than anticipated, despite the fact that, Plaid notwithstanding, almost nobody in Welsh politics wished to see the principality become an independent nation. The Tories were unanimously opposed to independence, but also viscerally averse to the idea of agreeing with Labour, on any grounds whatsoever. Their preferred solution was to leave Morgan to sort out his own mess, retiring to their usual summer quarters in Provence, Tuscany and Fishguard.

More vocal in their support, alas, were a motley assortment of fascists, eccentrics and Liberal Democrats. The Lib Dems, at least, were prevented from doing much damage by their stubborn anonymity. Less helpfully, the press took great delight in reporting every half-baked utterance of No campaigners such as Neil Hamilton and drink-addled squire Sir David "Dai" Llewellyn.[13] After John Redwood made some

---

[12] Several members of the Super Furry Animals were believed to be in favour of independence, but their public remarks on the subject were broadly incomprehensible.

[13] For all his faults, Dai Llewellyn deserves at least some measure of respect for having successfully sued John Etheridge for libel in 2003.

typically condescending remarks in an interview with the *Daily Telegraph*, Cardiff was soon awash with posters featuring Redwood's likeness anointed with the elegantly simple caption "Bastard".

One of the early surprises of the campaign was the extent to which the Welsh press threw its weight behind the Yes campaign. Opinion was split among the staff of the *Western Mail*, while the *Echo* largely chose to ignore the campaign until it entered its final days. *Y Cymro*, as might have been expected, was highly supportive. Perhaps more surprisingly, the *Argus* was fully behind the Yes campaign, as was the *Leader*, which published a string of editorials worthy of Gildas in an especially solemn mood. Even Red Dragon Radio decided to give free advertising spots to pro-independence messages, voiced by Neville Southall.

By mid-August, Rhodri Morgan was beginning to panic. Carwyn Jones was ordered to cut short his walking holiday in Ireland and return to Cardiff post-haste. Jane Hutt was recalled from her cottage in Tresaith, while Andrew Davies was eventually located in Bangkok and ordered to hurry home. Jane Davidson, on the other hand, flatly declined to get involved.[14] After a lengthy and occasionally ill-tempered debate, the Welsh Labour grandees decided upon a strategy which was almost quietist in its simplicity. In short, they agreed that their best hope was simply to shut up and wait it out, pinning all their hopes on a low turn-out at the polls. A strictly confidential memo was issued from the First Minister's office

---

[14] Davidson never quite recovered from the stress of the Shambo affair. The fact that the Yes campaign adopted Shambo as a mascot (T-shirts featuring his likeness were inescapable that summer) probably did not help.

advising all government ministers, Assembly members and staff to stop talking about the referendum in public.

The final weeks of the campaign played out in this bizarrely lop-sided manner, with the Yes brigade doing everything they could think of to drum up public interest while those in power steadfastly refused to acknowledge the situation, often to the point of absurdity.[15] The Welsh government had opened the door to the most momentous constitutional change since the Statute of Rhuddlan, then decided that they would rather not talk about it. While visiting a county show in Denbighshire, Carwyn Jones was pressed repeatedly for a comment on the referendum by local journalists. Jones blithely ignored their questions for an excruciating half hour, culminating in a farcical scene where the minister posed for photos with a lamb while chants of "Yes! Yes! Yes!" rang out all around. A few days later, with just one week to go before the vote, Welsh politics made one of its rare incursions into the national media. The producers of *Newsnight* had planned to include a ten-minute debate on the referendum towards the end of their programme, but the No campaign declined to send a representative. The panel thus consisted of an effervescent Ieuan Wyn Jones, a barely less excited Michael Sheen, and a cuddly toy sheep propped up on a chair to represent the absent unionists.[16] Jeremy Paxman's eyebrows were arched to new heights that evening.

---

[15] Readers are humbly referred to my own contemporary contribution, *'Leighton Andrews has a cold'*, published in the *New Welsh Review* (Vol XLII, No. 4). Despite some savage responses from certain quarters, I think the article holds up well.

[16] For several years afterwards, Carwyn Jones would be met with a chorus of "baaahs" whenever he was obliged to interact with the public in north Wales.

In spite of these and other embarrassments, polling data and internal research allowed Rhodri Morgan's inner circle to maintain their quiet optimism. Thursday 13th September 2007 was a warm and sunny day across much of Wales, a rare occurrence which Morgan was determined to interpret as a good omen. With many schools closed for the vote, he hoped that a sizeable portion of the electorate would choose to spend the day enjoying the late summer sunshine. Driving through the Vale of Glamorgan and observing the pub gardens doing brisk business that afternoon, Morgan began to feel increasingly confident. In keeping with Welsh Labour's strategy of obfuscation, there was no official No campaign headquarters and no plans were made for a victory party. Morgan, Jones, Davies and a huddle of trusted advisors instead ensconced themselves in the First Minister's office in Tŷ Hywel and awaited the exit polls.

The first peal of thunder rang out shortly after the polling stations closed that evening, when election officials declared the turn-out to be 50.22%. This announcement alone was enough to trigger an explosion of joy at Yes HQ, and indeed a swift foray to the nearby City Arms. Over at Tŷ Hywel nerves were beginning to fray, but these early jitters were assuaged as the first results began to roll in. By 11 o'clock a picture was already emerging, with No leading Yes by a steady margin of around 5%. Ties were loosened and bottles stealthily uncorked, as the mood among the First Minister's inner circle became more upbeat than it had been for many weeks.

The TV pundits were already calling a No victory by the time most people headed off to bed, but by midnight the tide had begun to turn. It soon became clear that many of the first polling stations to declare were located in the south-east, and only later in the evening did results begin to trickle in from the far corners of west and north Wales. Slowly but inexorably, the two sides drew closer and closer until they were finally separated by a dramatic swing in the final hour. When Ceredigion declared at 1 o'clock, the numbers of the board were unequivocal: Yes 50.3% – No 49.7%.

There was stunned silence in the BBC studio, as a visibly exhausted Jamie Owen struggled to form a coherent sentence. A similar sense of shock and awe gripped the ill-prepared guests on S4C and ITV, while the producers desperately awaited images of the scenes on the ground in Cardiff. It is impossible to say exactly what went on inside the FM's offices that evening, as none of those present have ever accepted to speak about it publicly. Rhodri Morgan, of course, took his own version of events to the grave.

The BBC, ITV and S4C had all sent out small camera crews to get the initial reactions of the winning party, and all three had set up camp in Cardiff Bay to await Rhodri Morgan's closing remarks. When the bombshell finally dropped, Morgan refused to leave his office. Just as he had stubbornly attempted to ignore the chain of events he had set in motion, he now seemed determined to avoid their unthinkable realisation. By the time the outside broadcast vans made it up to Westgate Street, they were greeted by scenes of pandemonium. The student volunteers erupted onto the streets of Cardiff, spraying beer into the night air and posing for photos with the statue of Nye

Bevan. But even as Womanby Street resounded to the strains of 'Men of Harlech', the most prominent Yes campaigners were somehow unavailable for comment. In spite of their initial jubilation, it rapidly became clear that the independentists had not prepared for this outcome.

―――

Friday 14th September should have marked the dawn of an uncertain and unprecedented future for Wales. Sporadic celebrations erupted in Wrexham, Machynlleth and Carmarthen, but Cardiff remained eerily quiet. Journalists gathered outside the new Senedd building, but there was no Assembly business scheduled for that day and the place was almost entirely deserted. Behind the scenes, however, the atmosphere was one of barely contained chaos. In a series of frantic meetings, civil servants and special advisers workshopped all manner of excuses, pretexts and ruses. The most widely backed solution was to declare that the referendum was not legally binding, since the government had never actually specified what independence would entail. More radical elements set about concocting stories of voter fraud, sprinkled with allegations of interference by English entryists and the ever-dreaded second-homeowners.[17] Ultimately, these far-fetched excuses would go unused. Within a few days of the vote it had become clear that there was to be no Welsh Revolution after all.

―――――――――――――――――――

[17] Etheridge has suggested that some members of Welsh Labour welcomed the result and began to prepare a formal declaration of independence, a tale so improbable it merits a new entry in the Aarne-Thompson-Uther Index.

The Rugby World Cup provided a welcome distraction on the Saturday, although Morgan himself felt it better to stay away, watching the match from the safety of his study with a bottle of Penderyn to hand. Carwyn Jones was sent to deputise, perhaps because of his proven ability to ignore questions while grinning steadfastly for the cameras. The whereabouts of Ieuan Wyn Jones, however, remained a mystery.

By Monday, Morgan had still not shown his face in public and the government had declined even to acknowledge the referendum result. In this respect they remained true to their strategy of wilful ignorance, but much more surprising was the lack of media scrutiny or reaction. Radio Cymru's phone-ins were unusually busy over the weekend, but talk of the referendum rapidly made way for discussions of the rugby result and news from elsewhere. Oddly, Monday's newspapers contained virtually no mention of the events of the previous Thursday. The *Western Mail* ran an opinion piece calling for calm and reflection, and the *Argus* contained a handful of readers' letters on the subject, but that was the full extent of the press coverage. Circumstances playing out beyond Wales's borders undoubtedly played a role: over the weekend, long queues had been forming outside branches of Northern Rock as the first run on a British bank in 150 years rapidly gathered pace. The tabloids, meanwhile, had no shortage of sports and celebrity gossip to occupy their pages, not to mention the latest ruthless speculation on the whereabouts of Madeleine McCann.

On Wednesday, Peter Hain visited Cardiff in the company of Baron Kinnock, ostensibly to mark the beginning of the academic year at the university. During a brief press conference the pair alluded several times to the referendum, apparently in anticipation of a flood of questions. The thin scattering of journalists in attendance failed to take the bait, and Kinnock and Hain returned to Westminster perplexed but thoroughly relieved.

Throughout the days and weeks after September 13th, the senior leadership of Plaid Cymru were conspicuous by their absence from all events involving television cameras. They also appeared to be observing some form of social media blackout, a silence which extended to the party's rank and file membership. On the streets of Cardiff, even the Young Turks of the Yes Cymru campaign seemed to have melted away. He may have miscalculated the rest, but Rhodri Morgan got one thing right: the independentists were not prepared for independence, not in the slightest.

On Thursday, a full week after the vote, Morgan returned to work as if nothing had happened. The First Minister spent the morning at the Senedd attending to parliamentary business, before visiting a yoghurt factory in Risca in the afternoon. Sporadic, isolated acts of protest would continue for a few weeks, but were mostly limited to handwritten Yes Cymru signs brandished in Morgan's general vicinity as he returned to his usual round of public appearances.

The most striking exception, and incidentally one of the most stunningly incongruous events in the whole of Welsh history, came on Friday 28 September when a militant independentist self-immolated in front of the Senedd building. Unhappily for the young incendiary, he chose to make his ultimate sacrifice at 10 o'clock on a blustery autumn morning, and there were few witnesses. No photographic record of the event has survived, but the few first-hand accounts available describe the heroic efforts of a passer-by to extinguish the flames with the only materials to hand, namely a can of Diet Coke and an M&S anorak. Alas, her efforts were in vain.

The man was later identified as Llewelyn Griffiths of Carmarthen; the body itself was charred beyond recognition, but police were able to identify Griffiths because his car was double parked nearby. He left a manifesto of sorts, but the colourful language employed throughout meant that it was effectively unpublishable.[18]

In some respects this human blaze marked the climax of the Yes movement, and also its effective conclusion. Much like the almost-historic moment he sought to salvage, the ultimate sacrifice of this deranged nationalist was rapidly consigned to the oblivion of collective disinterest. Fellow independentists affixed a plaque near the entrance to the Senedd commemorating Griffiths' desperate act, but it has since been replaced with a sign bearing the more functional injunction "No Skateboarding".

On Monday 1st October, Senedd sessions resumed as if nothing had happened. A few months later, the Assembly government quietly published legal advice stating that the referendum had never been approved by the Parliament in Westminster, and thus had no real value. In reality, this constitutional chicanery

---

[18] Readers are advised to seek out this text in the original Welsh. The English translation published by L. Ramsay is of shockingly poor quality. And who supervised his doctoral thesis? You guessed it: John Etheridge. Just give up, John, that research fellowship is mine and you know it.

was far from necessary. By that time the people of Wales had already decided to indulge in a strange form of mass amnesia, and indeed most of them had forgotten that they had even voted, if indeed they had.

———

Perhaps the dramatic death of Llewelyn Griffiths can help us to understand why even the nationalists were so keen to pretend that the referendum never happened. Despite years of campaigning for independence (half-heartedly, admittedly), they had failed to properly consider the consequences of a constitutional revolution on this scale. The disconnect between a lifelong desire and the bitter disappointment of its realisation must have come as a brutal, disorienting shock to many. The cognitive dissonance of it all was too much for poor Griffiths, who appears to have lost his mind. Here was an event so seismic, so astonishing, that people were neither willing nor able to comprehend it. This was true of the public at large, but also of those closest to the cause. The idea of putting the referendum result into practice, of laying the foundations for an independent, sovereign Welsh nation, still seemed impossibly remote. Imagine the work involved! Much better to remain a country of dead heroes and dead saints.

Author Biographies

Brennig Davies is from the Vale of Glamorgan. He won the inaugural BBC Young Writers Award in 2015, the Crown at the Urdd Eisteddfod 2019, and was previously shortlisted for the Rhys Davies Short Story Competition in 2021. His work has appeared in *London Magazine* and *Poetry Wales*, and has been broadcast on BBC Radio 4. In 2023 he was chosen as one of the Hay Festival's Writers at Work.

Morgan Davies writes about landscape, place, and nature. He has a master's degree in creative writing from the University of Edinburgh with Distinction, and a PhD in creative writing from Aberystwyth University for which he was awarded a departmental postgraduate studentship. Morgan has written for *New Welsh Review* and *Nation.Cymru*, and his short stories set in rural Wales have been published and performed. His debut novel, *The Burning Bracken*, was published in 2022 by Victorina Press. He lives in mid Wales with his wife and children.

Kamand Kojouri is an Assistant Professor of English at the American University in Dubai. She holds a creative writing MA from City, University of London and PhD from Swansea University. Her MA novel was shortlisted for the Peters Fraser + Dunlop award, and she has been featured on the BBC, *El País*, and *The Irish Times*. All the royalties from her poetry collections, *The Eternal Dance* (2018) and *God, Does Humanity Exist?* (2020), are donated to The Trevor Project and Child

Foundation. She also funds tree-planting initiatives in Sub-Saharan Africa, with 2,920 trees planted to date.

Dave Lewis is a writer, poet and photographer from Cilfynydd. He read zoology at Cardiff University, taught biology in Kenya and loves to travel. He runs the International Welsh Poetry Competition and the Poetry Book Awards. His epic poem, *Roadkill*, outlines the class struggle, while his collection, *Going Off Grid*, warns of the dangers of digital capitalism. His latest release, *Algorithm*, dips into AI, war, nature, race, love and travel. He has produced a crime thriller trilogy and the highly-acclaimed novel, *The Welsh Man*. He likes dogs, elephants and real ale.

Website: www.david-lewis.co.uk

Kapu Lewis is a Welsh writer and poet with autism, and is deeply interested in using storytelling to explore mental health and neurodiversity. Kapu started her career as a journalist, interning at Pembrokeshire's *Western Telegraph* and the *Carmarthen Journal*, and later attending the Cardiff School of Journalism. She now consults for TV and film.

Kapu grew up in Carmarthenshire and now splits her time between London and west Wales. Her work has been published by Epoque Press, *The Berlin Literary Review*, *Handwritten & Co.*, *The Mechanics' Institute Review*, Erro Press and *The Menteur*.

Website: www.kapulewis.com

Lloyd Lewis is a Welsh writer and translator. Born and raised in Glamorgan, after studying French literature at university he decided to spend a year in the south-west of France. He has thus far failed to return, and currently lives in Bordeaux with his wife and daughters.

Polly Manning grew up in Carmarthenshire and lives in Swansea. She writes short stories about the everyday lives of people in south Wales, and her non-fiction work has appeared in publications including *VICE*, *Planet*, the *Western Mail*, and *The Welsh Agenda*. In 2022 she was awarded the White Pube Writers' Grant, and is a soon-to-be graduate of the MA Creative Writing: Prose Fiction programme at the University of East Anglia, where she was the 2023-24 Annabel Abbs Scholar. She is currently working on her first collection of short stories.

Born and bred in Brymbo, a small village near Wrexham in north Wales, **Siân Marlow** moved to Reading in 2010, where she lives with her husband and son and their two big dogs. A Modern Languages graduate of St David's University College in Lampeter, specialising in Swedish and German, Siân started her own small translation company as a way of indulging her passion for the written word. She is currently working on a Master's degree in creative writing at the University of Reading and has just completed her debut novel, *World Without End*. Besides her love of books, Siân loves choral singing and long walks with her dogs.

Keza O'Neill grew up in Aberystwyth. She studied French in Sheffield and Quebec and gained an MA in Creative Writing with Distinction from the Open University. A qualified coach-mentor, Keza spent fifteen years working in People Operations, supporting clients worldwide. Having lived and worked in six countries, she's interested in relationships between people and places and the significance of 'home' in shaping identity.

Keza's story 'Lucky Strike' won the Sansom Award and placed third in the Bristol Short Story Prize. Longlisted for the

Bath Short Story Award, the CWA Debut Dagger and the Lucy Cavendish Fiction Prize, she lives in Bristol because home is just across the bridge.

Tanya Pengelly is a Welsh writer living in Warwickshire, England. She holds a PhD in creative writing and the narratology of friendship, and has a great interest in traditional performance storytelling, having served as chair of the board for Beyond the Border Wales's International Storytelling Festival. Her writing strays between literary psychological fiction and speculative fiction, but is always rooted in how the landscape around us informs the stories we tell ourselves. In 2024, Tanya won the Robert Day Award for Fiction, and her stories have appeared in several anthologies and literary magazines.

Website: www.tanyapengelly.com

Anthony Shapland grew up in the Rhymney Valley. He was part of the Representing Wales cohort in 2022, the same year he was included in *Cree: The Rhys Davies Short Story Award Anthology* (Parthian). He appears in the anthologies *Cymru & I*, (Seren / Inclusive Journalism) and *(un)common* (Lucent Dreaming). He was a Hay Writer at Work in 2023 and his fiction, 'Feathertongue', for Radio 4's Short Works series will be broadcast in Autumn 2024. His debut novel *A Room Above a Shop* will be published by Granta in Spring 2025.

Jo Verity was born in Newport and has lived in London, Cwmbran and Cardiff. She wrote her first short story twenty-five years ago and in 2003, 'Rapid Eye Movement' won the Richard & Judy Short Story Competition.

Over the years, Jo's stories have been broadcast on Radio 4, won competitions, including the *Western Mail*'s short story prize and appeared in anthologies such as *The Bus Stop Scheherazade* (Cinnamon Press). 'Trespass' was a runner up in the 2011 Rhys Davies Competition.

Alongside short fiction, Jo has published six novels with Honno Press and is currently grappling with the ending of her seventh.

PARTHIAN

RHYS DAVIES

RHYS DAVIES: SELECTED STORIES

Rhys Davies

"Gently wrapped, these stylish perceptive tales have centres as hard as steel, and are all the better for it."
– *William Trevor*, The Guardian

£8.99 / PB
978-1-912109-78-4

RHYS DAVIES: A WRITER'S LIFE

Meic Stephens

"This is a delightful book, which is itself a social history in its own right, and funny."
– The Spectator

£11.99 / PB
978-1-912109-96-8

PARTHIAN   Fiction

Take a Bite:
The Rhys Davies Short Story
Award Anthology

ISBN 978-1-913640-63-7
£9.99 • Paperback

THE TWELVE WINNERS OF THE 2021
RHYS DAVIES SHORT STORY AWARD

Cree:
The Rhys Davies Short Story
Award Anthology

ISBN 978-1-914595-23-3
£10 • Paperback

THE TWELVE WINNERS OF THE 2022
RHYS DAVIES SHORT STORY AWARD

Harvest:
The Rhys Davies Short Story
Award Anthology

ISBN 978-1-914595-74-5
£10 • Paperback

THE TWELVE WINNERS OF THE 2023
RHYS DAVIES SHORT STORY AWARD

PARTHIAN　Short Stories

Figurehead

CARLY HOLMES
ISBN 978-1-912681-77-8
£10.00 • Paperback

'Through beautiful, rhythmic prose *Figurehead* weaves a sequence of stories that are strange, captivating, and unforgettable.' – Wales Arts Review

Whatever Happened to Rick Astley?

BRYONY RHEAM
ISBN: 978-1-914595-14-1
£10.00 • Paperback

'Bryony Rheam's short stories are skilled, perfectly formed, and compelling ... a deeply satisfying collection...'
– Karen Jennings

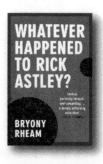

Local Fires

JOSHUA JONES
ISBN 978-1-913640-59-0
£10.00 • Paperback

'In this stunning series of interconnected tales, fires both literal and metaphorical blaze together to herald the emergence of a singular new Welsh literary voice.'

Men Alone

ÖZGÜR UYANIK
ISBN: 978-1-914595-82-0
£10.00 • Paperback

'This wry, moving, and beautifully crafted collection of stories is a rich and multilayered meditation on aloneness.'
– Tristan Hughes

PARTHIAN

Fiction

Fox Bites

LLOYD MARKHAM
ISBN 978-1-914595-17-2
£10.99 • Paperback

'A bold, ambitious new novel from Cardiff-based Lloyd Markham... a dark and genuinely gripping work of fantasy horror.'
– Joshua Rees

Unspeakable Beauty

GEORGIA CARYS WILLIAMS
ISBN 978-1-914595-42-4
£10.99 • Paperback

'A truly impressive achievement from a rising star of Welsh literature.'
– Gosia Buzzanca

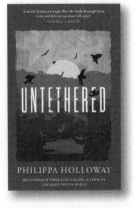

Untethered

PHILIPPA HOLLOWAY
ISBN 978-1-914595-85-1
£10.00 • Paperback

'A mood of ancient magic flits like birds through these eerie and delicate modern folk tales.'
– Samira Ahmed